After The Storm

by

Natalie P. Jenkins

I have tried to recreate events, locales and conversations from my memories of them. In order to maintain their anonymity in some instances I have changed the names of individuals and places, I may have changed some identifying characteristics and details such as physical properties, occupations and places of residence.

Paper Back Edition 12/20

ISBN 9798631154568

Copyright © 2020 Natalie P. Jenkins

Natalie P. Jenkins asserts the moral right to be identified as the author of this work. All rights reserved in all media. No part of this publication may be reproduced, stored in a retrieval system, or transmitted, in any form, or by any means, electronic, mechanical, photocopying, recording or otherwise, without the prior written permission of the author and/or publisher.

After The Storm

by

Natalie P. Jenkins

To Brandon. Thank you for showing me that love was not impossible to have again and for putting up with my complaining throughout my writing process.

Chapter 1

Natalie stood at the altar of the Salyersville First Baptist Church, looking down inside of a beautifully polished casket. Her eyes were filled with tears as she leaned in carefully against his ear and whispered "I love you so much." She grasped his right hand and pulled it close to her. "I can't believe he's really gone," she thought, as she began to weep, praying to God that this was all just a bad dream. The pastor of the church saw her distress and approached her, comforting her as she silently sobbed. He put his arm around Natalie and pulled her into a hug. "You're worried that you're going to be alone, aren't you?" He asked.

Natalie looked up at him, her eyes red and wet with tears, "Yes," she nodded.

"I can't leave you alone, if I did, Jason would be waiting for me at the gates of heaven," he laughed, patting her back to get her to calm down.

Natalie managed to crack a smile at his weird sense of humor. Jason was protective over Natalie, he loved her so much that coming back from Heaven was plausible.

She took a deep breath and turned away from the casket, returning back to her seat. She put her hands on her knees, revealing her diamond engagement ring to people around her. The large diamonds sparkled in the morning sunlight, shining through the stained glass windows. She looked down at the now grim reminder of reality.

She took a deep breath and turned away from the casket, returning back to her seat. She put her hands on her knees, revealing her diamond engagement ring to people around her. The diamonds sparkled in the morning sunlight shining through the stained glass windows. She looked down at the ring, a now grim reminder of reality.

Natalie stood up for the last time and felt a brush up against her arm. Another preacher, who held the position of apostle in the church, was standing beside of her. He prayed over her. "God loves you, Natalie," he assured her as he finished praying. He looked at her with a sympathetic look, helping Natalie walk away as the service came to a close.

Singing began in the sanctuary, causing her to break down. She realized that these were her final moments with Jason on this Earth. Blake came up behind her and put his hand on her back. His emotions overtook him, as he looked upon his best friend for the last time. He cried and placed a picture inside the casket, next to Jason's head of the two of them celebrating their college graduation together.

    Blake was broken. The man, who was the closest thing he had to a brother, was gone. He pulled himself together, and tried his best to keep his composure to be a support for Natalie. He left the sanctuary and went to stand with the other firefighters that he and Jason worked with, leaving Natalie alone to go find her parents.

    Natalie felt like everyone's eyes were on her. She is a person who hates attention and always has. Natalie was shy and interacting with others was difficult for her. She hid her face, but noticed that people were still watching, giving her anxiety. People were whispering things about her, others gave glances so sharp that it could've killed. She wanted to hide, but there was nowhere to go. Jason was the opposite of Natalie. He was outgoing and loved attention. The two of them complimented each other very well.

Natalie shivered in the cold January wind, as she stood behind the casket in front of the church. "What is taking so long?" She questioned, growing impatient with the wait. Finally, a young man dressed in a uniform of a white polo shirt and khakis, came outside carrying a black case in his right hand. He opened up the case, after struggling with a lock, and took out a trumpet, and began to play taps.

Natalie's heart broke as the brassy sound of the trumpet pierced through her ears and heart. Silence soon fell over the crowd, and the crowd dispersed into their vehicles. The silence was soon interrupted by the roaring sound of helicopters flying over. The last call went out over the radio.

"Last call for Unit Number 948, assistant chaplain, Jason Tackett. We'll take it from here,"

Natalie looked up at the sky, watching the fly over. As The firefighters saluted the casket again before it was placed into the back of a white hearse. Natalie stood by her car door, barely holding herself together. Natalie was so full of faith. She was known by her close family and relatives as a devout Christian, but now her faith was shaken.

The sky was a beautiful bright blue and the sun was very bright. It looked like spring. One of the most beautiful days Natalie had seen in a while. It just didn't seem right.

Jason's tear filled Fiancé, sat down in the front passengers seat of her car. All the pain she was holding back came flowing out in tears.

"This isn't fair! I shouldn't have to be here," she screamed. She laid her head up against the window and tears rolled down her cheeks. She sat there alone inside the car, and she was thankful for those few moments alone. She finally felt like she could breathe.

"The hardest day of my life is over," she thought, still sobbing as she was trying to look at the positives of her bleak situation.

    Natalie looked up and saw her father walking towards the vehicle. A strong rush of relief came over her when he sat down in the drivers seat, while her mother got into the backseat. She was close with her parents, and they made her feel slightly at ease.

"Do you want to take pictures of the flag?" Natalie's mother asked from the backseat pointing towards the large American flag hanging between two fire trucks.

"No! I don't want to remember any of this!" Natalie replied, with her voice cracking.

    The wind blew the flag and the bright winter sun shone on it, illuminating its beautiful colors. As the car kept approaching the cemetery, Natalie's heart sank.

She turned her head to look out the window of all the people lined up and down the streets, watching the funeral procession go by. She was amazed at the amount of people who standing beside the road in honor of her late fiancé.

"Jason lived more life in 26 years than I have in 50," her father said.

"Everyone loved him," Natalie added, as she turned her focus back to the road. Trying to think about anything else other than her reality.

    Natalie and her parents arrived at the burial location. The family cemetery was at the very top of a steep hill in the backwoods of Kentucky. There was only one very small narrow gravel road leading to it. Natalie struggled to walk through the thick mud and frozen gravel.

"Natalie!" A male voice said from behind her, surprised. "How are you holding up?"

Natalie turned around to see Blake standing next to her. Natalie looked at him and just sighed.

"I understand completely," he said, placing his arm around Natalie, rubbing her back to comfort her as he cried with her.

Natalie made her way into the cemetery gates, along with Blake following behind her. The preacher was the last one to make it. He got out of the car and approached Natalie. "Do you want me to help you?" He asked seeing Natalie struggle to walk. She shook her head no. Jason was taken out of the back of the hearse. Natalie stood and watched in horror as they slowly carried the casket through the gates of the cemetery. The Firefighters lined up around the gates, ushering in the casket.

Natalie stood to the side, looking down into the deep hole that was in front of her. The thoughts of Jason going into the cold hard ground disturbed her greatly.

"Why him Lord?" She questioned, wondering why God would take away one of his servants. Someone who worshipped Him endlessly.

Natalie's heart was pounding with every second that passed by. Tears started to well up in her eyes, realizing that this was the end, there was no coming back from the grave. Taps was played for a final time. The preacher walked up behind the casket and took his bible out of his coat pocket that had notes written in it. "Today, we are here to honor the life of this brave soul. A Good man who was taken from us far too soon. Thank you to each one of you, who came. This is a sad occasion for all of us," The preacher said, then paused for a moment before speaking again.
"In the midnight hours of Sunday morning, we experienced such an incredible loss. We lost a son, a fiancé, a friend and teacher. Every time I asked him to do something at church, he never let me down. We will

all miss him, but we must remember that he has went home to be with the Lord and is in the presence of his savior,"

The preacher stopped for a moment. Taking a handkerchief out of his coat pocket to blow his nose and wipe his tears away. Jason was a close friend of his and he had taken up with Natalie. They had been through a lot together from mentoring Jason through his call to preach, to praying for the perfect woman to come into his life. The presence of Natalie in Jason's life was considered a miracle by many.

The preacher quickly regained his composure. He finished reading some scripture and said a closing prayer.

"Heavenly Father, we thank you for revealing to us what lies beyond death, for giving us the Holy Spirit to comfort us, and for the Holy scriptures that you have authenticated through many wonderful evidences and making them incontrovertible evidence of the resurrection of Jesus Christ. Thank you, therefore, that our Lord Jesus Christ has prepared a place for those who have put their faith in him and that he is personally coming back to raise us from the grave. Now for the family and friends, we ask that you would comfort and strengthen them in the days ahead. Help the family and friends and draw strength and comfort from you. In Jesus' name we pray, Amen,"

The prayer finished, and wind began to blow through the trees only where they were standing. Natalie cried quietly, trying not to draw attention to herself. "What am I going to do?" Natalie thought, feeling hopeless as tears rolled down her cheeks.

The service was finally over. Natalie took a deep breath and relaxed a little. What was once going to be a wonderful and happy marriage, was now just a memory of what almost was.

Memories were all that she had left of him. Only memories, mere images of the past that were stored in her mind. It wasn't the same as having him alive. There was a void in her soul so deep, that no one could fill. the man who held her every night, was being put into the ground for an eternity.

Suddenly, Natalie felt someone grab her arm. She looked around to discover that it was the preacher. He pulled Natalie over to the side and put his arm around her "Listen, you call me or message me anytime you want. I'll even come to your house if you want me to," he said, reassuring her as he helped her walk back to her car. She didn't make it very far before she was stopped again by Jason's grandfather. "Wait, Natalie! You forgot to take a rose," He said as he cut off a rose from Jason's casket. Everyone that was close to him took a rose from his casket just before he was lowered into the ground.

She sat down in the car, looking down at the beautiful red rose in her hand. She was still running off the high of being newly engaged and dealing with shock and trauma. She was totally numb.

Reality had not completely set in yet, but she knew that her life was going to have to be rebuilt from the ground up. "Where do I start? What do I do first?" She thought.

Her mother opened the car door, interrupting her train of thought. Her father got in next, and started the vehicle. "Natalie, we're going to go visit with your grandparents for a while,"

"Okay," Natalie groaned. She was frustrated and wanted nothing more than to just go home and rest. She was mentally and physically exhausted, and hadn't slept in days."I just want to go home," she thought.

 Natalie became silent and kept her thoughts to herself. She had no choice, because nothing she said or did would make her mother change her mind. She was screaming on the inside, knowing that she was going to be there for a while. Natalie came into her grandmother's house and sat down in the living room alone, trying to avoid interacting with them. She laid her head down on the couch, enjoying the peace and quiet for a moments.

"Natalie, you need to eat something," her mother yelled from the kitchen.

"I'm not hungry," she groaned as she put her head back down on the arm rest.

Her grandmother saw that she was sitting alone, so she invited her to come sit at the kitchen table with them. Eventually, she agreed just to get them to stop bothering her.

"Mom, can we please just go home?" She asked angrily, trying not to cry.

"In a minute," She replied.

Natalie was frustrated and got up from the table, after sitting there for a few moments, and went back to the living room where she would be alone again. The noise of her family talking aggravated her to no end. She laid down on the couch, covering her head with a pillow to block the noise. Normally, she would have enjoyed spending time with them, but the joy she once had in her heart was gone.

Darkness fell that evening and Natalie could not take her mind off Jason. She kept checking her phone for text messages from him out of habit from doing that everyday. Each time she checked, there was only disappointment.

"He just texted me the other day, and now he's gone. It's so hard to believe," Natalie thought, reading through her old messages from Jason and sobbing. Her last message from him was about Ice Cream and when she read it, she smiled. "He was something else," she thought as she put her phone away and tried not to think about him.

The next morning, the sun was out and shining bright. There were four rainbows throughout the gorgeous blue sky. "Why can't I share this beautiful sight with Jason?" Natalie thought as she overheard her family talking about it. Her parents took it as a sign from God, but Natalie was disgusted by the sight. She closed up the kitchen curtains, hiding it from her view

She sat down on the couch and looked down at the floor. "I don't have anyone to support me anymore," she thought, feeling helpless and desperate for some kind of help. The one person she wanted to talk to, was the one she didn't have. There simply was no one left on this Earth who could love and understand her like Jason did. That morning, Natalie realized that she had to go on without him and it seemed impossible.

Natalie laid back on the brown plush couch and examined her life, or what was left of it per say. "I'll never love anyone ever again," she said. Everything in her life was just a mess of failures, heartbreak and sorrows. Natalie no longer had motivation or will to live. There was no point in living anymore. All that was left of her once happy and vibrant life was memories.

She went to her room and hid underneath the bed covers, making herself comfortable in hopes that she would be able to get a nap. As she began to drift off to sleep, her mind wandered. "How am I gonna move on from this?" She thought. Starting over again was the most terrifying thing she had ever faced in her life. "I don't need to think about this right now," she reassured herself.

Natalie was resting comfortably when she was interrupted by her mother.

"Natalie, come in here, there's someone here to see you," she said. Natalie groaned and turned over, stretched then got up, angry, and realized that she hadn't had much of a nap at all. Frustrated by the guest, she quickly put some clothes on and came into the living room.

Natalie grabbed her phone out of habit "I don't even need this thing anymore," she said. However, this time, she did have a message from his best friend, who was checking on her. The message was thoughtful, but it reminded her of how truly alone she was. Natalie doesn't do well alone. Her whole life, she had been surrounded by people who loved and cared for her. She left her phone on her bed and didn't respond. She didn't want to talk to anybody at that moment. She left her bedroom and walked into the kitchen, holding back tears. It was some of her mother's friends who brought her some food and gifts.

"How are you doing?" One of them asked.

"About as good as one can do in this situation," she responded, biting her tongue to keep from giving a smart Alec response. She held her head down trying to avoid contact as the blonde haired woman handed Natalie a small gift bag.

"I know it's painful now, but it will get better in time. It always does," she said, as she handed the bag to her.

"I feel like I've lost a part of me," Natalie said, as she sat down at the table.

"That's because you did lose a part of you," the blonde haired woman responded.

Natalie sat there at a loss for words. They did not know what to say to her. They wanted to make her feel better, but no words could help. Everything they said just made it worse. Natalie put her hands over her eyes, resting her head in her hands, wishing the misery she was in would go away. She didn't know what else to do, other than talk to someone she knew she could trust. She excused herself left the table, when she had an idea. She went and picked up her phone and began texting her and Jason's church pastor.

Finally, later that evening, she received a message back, giving her a little bit of hope and putting a smile on her face.

"You didn't do anything, it was just an attack from Satan," He responded.

He called her immediately and they talked for a while, giving Natalie a chance to blow off some steam. It wasn't long until the tears started flowing again. Embarrassed, she apologized to the pastor several times for having to hear her cry for so long. "How do I find someone else?" She asked

The pastor laughed. "Well, at least you've not completely given up," he assured her, seeing hope in her future and a determination to rebuild her life.

"Have you considered going to see a therapist?" He interrupted.

"Yeah, I have,"

"Good, you're a smart young woman. Jason was right to choose you. Don't worry too much about moving on, just focus on Natalie right now,"

"How in the world do I focus on myself right now?" Natalie asked. She hadn't focused on herself in so long. Her life was about Jason and building their relationship together. Everyone always came first in her world.

"Right now, you just need to focus on putting God first, and the rest will fall into place. Have you read through your bible any today?" He asked.

"Yeah, I have,"

"Keep reading the psalms for comfort," he reminded her as the conversation came to a close. Feeling better, she hung up the phone and drifted slowly off to sleep with a new outlook.

Chapter 2

Natalie was running as fast as she could down the yellow line on the small winding country road known as elk creek. There was a man standing and directing traffic and she spoke to him.

"Where's he at?" She yelled in panic.

"He's over there," he said, pointing to an ambulance that was waiting in a nearby field.

"Is he okay?" She asked, gasping for breath.

The paramedic patted Natalie's back in an attempt to comfort her. "It's okay, just stay calm," he said, rubbing her back before finally telling her what was going on. "Both of his legs are broken and there's some internal injuries. When they got to him he was unconscious but still breathing, as of now he's stable but he's in a lot of pain. We're airlifting him to the nearest hospital,"

Natalie wailed upon hearing the news. She stumbled, almost falling to the ground. Something wasn't right, and she knew it. She took a few steps back from the wreckage and looked around, not quite processing everything that was going on.

"We just went and got her wedding dress today," Natalie's mother spoke up, adding to her panic.

She couldn't do anything but scream in horror at the situation unfolding before her eyes. She had no idea what was happening and she knew this was out of her control. A firefighter who was working the scene came over to her and tried to keep her calm.

"It's going to be alright. I promise you, he's in good hands," he said.

Natalie began to shiver from the cold night air. It was the coldest night the county had seen in a while. It was four degrees, her fingers were going numb and she had no coat on, just a thin gray long sleeved t-shirt. She was encouraged to go sit in her car, as her mother walked down to talk to the multitude of people who were around the back of the ambulance. Most of which were Jason's friends.

"Lord, save his life. I can't live without him. I'll take him anyway I can get him, just don't take him away from me!" She prayed, sitting in the front passengers seat looking out the window. She knew that something was seriously wrong by them not letting her see him. She continued to pray, knowing that only God could help him at this point. She prayed the hardest she'd ever prayed in her life, and stopped when she looked up and saw her mother approaching the car.

"I talked to them, and they said he's stable. They also checked his blood sugar and it was good. They told me that the boy who hit him was Dustin Cottle, another boy in the fire department," Her mother explained.

"Oh God don't say that! He was probably drunk, that's all he ever does is drink," Natalie said as her heart sank to her stomach.

After about thirty minutes of chest compressions, the ambulance doors opened. The loud sounds of the helicopter blades soon filled the air. The bright yellow medical helicopter made landfall in the field next to the ambulance. There were ten men carrying Jason. They stood close around him covering most of his body. He appeared lifeless and he was already gray from what little she could see. Reality was setting in that it wasn't good.

Natalie's cousin Ron, who was working the scene approached her as the helicopter left.

"Is he going to he alright?" Natalie asked.

"Ah now, he's hurt," Ron said. Natalie collapsed and any hope of him surviving was gone.

"Let's go!" She screamed at her mother, as the helicopter began to lift up off the ground. Both of them ran to the car and sped to the hospital as fast as they could.

When they crossed the pike county line, Natalie got a phone call.

" I can't answer it," she said handing it to her mother.

Her mother answered the phone, and her tone instantly changed. Natalie felt a jolt go through her chest as she prepared herself to hear the worst.

"He's dead," her mother informed her.

"No!" She screamed, and threw her body on the dash board of the car.

Suddenly, Natalie's eyes flew open. Gasping for air, she jolted up in bed. "Oh my God, it was just a dream," She said, clenching her chest and breathing heavily. She rubbed her forehead, that was covered in beads of sweat, as she tried to calm herself down. She reached over to her lamp on the night stand and fumbled around until she found the switch. The light came on, and she breathed a sigh of relief. "It was only a nightmare," she thought.

It troubled her deeply, leaving her with an uneasy feeling as the events of the night Jason died replayed in her head. Unable to go back to sleep, Natalie checked her phone to see what time it was. It was five in the morning on the fourteenth of January. Today marked exactly one week since Jason passed away. She leaned up against the headboard of her bed. Holding back tears, she thought of things she could do to get her mind off of him.

After a while, Natalie laid back down and stared up at the ceiling, focusing on the patterns of the plaster. She had never felt pain like this before. She was completely broken. Not only did she loose the most important person in her life, but she also lost a relationship, a marriage and a future.

"This isn't going to last forever," she told herself, trying to make herself feel better. Laying there, on her back, she thought of everything that could have been between the two of them. Eventually, she drifted back off to sleep.

When she woke up, his death still did not feel real. Her body and mind refused to accept that Jason was gone. Natalie struggled with that concept, often wondering why it was her that God was punishing.

The bright winter sun peeked through the blinds covering her bedroom window. She groaned as she made herself sit up on the edge of the bed. It was well past noon. She rubbed her forehead and stretched. "I'm forever going to be known as that poor little girl whose fiancé was killed in a car accident," Natalie thought.

She stood up and slowly came into the living room where the rest of her family was. "Good morning," her mother said.

"It's not morning anymore," Natalie added as she flopped down on the couch. She picked up her phone and saw a lot of messages from people who were checking on her. Some were thoughtful and made her feel a little better. Except for the few messages from men wanting to date her.

She pushed her feelings to the side, and tried to focus on something else. Ignoring her feelings were easier than dealing with them. If she could ignore the feelings, then she wouldn't have to be sad. That Saturday, she was feeling better, though something felt wrong. "Why am I so happy today?" She questioned, thinking she was loosing her mind. For the first time in a whole week, she did not cry.

Natalie was going to force herself, that day, to start a new routine. She was bound and determined to live normally, even if it was just for a day. She took advantage of her positive mood. She actually felt like spending time with her family for the first time in a week. Her black cat brushed up against her legs, grabbing her attention.

"Hi kitty cat," she said, bending down to pet him. She picked him up and held him close to her.

"What am I going to do to keep myself busy?" She asked.

"You could start a hobby," her mother suggested.

She paused for a moment, and thought about all the things she could do to keep herself busy. "I could start playing guitar again," she thought, but there were painful memories attached to that too.

After thinking for a few moments, she considered redecorating. It was something she loved to do, and it needed to be done. Her bedroom was like that of a child's, colorful and covered in butterflies.

"Would you consider letting me redecorate?" She asked.

"We'll think about it," her father said.

When night fell that evening, her hope was beginning to dwindle. Natalie felt an overload of emotions that she pushed to the back of her mind earlier. She finally got motivation to get up off the couch and went to take a bath to relax. The feelings that Natalie was experiencing were foreign to her. She never thought that she would get to a point where taking her own life seemed like the only way out. "I will never say that people struggling with suicide are crazy ever again," she thought, as she sank down into the bath water, feeling pain, she didn't even know was possible.

Most days, Natalie wanted to hide away from the world. Other days, she wanted the world to end. Avoiding the pain was easier than facing the pain. "If I die, I won't have to suffer like this anymore," she thought, knowing that would be the end to all of her problems. Her life simply was not worth living anymore.

Natalie got out of the tub, dried off and went to lie down in her bed. Her hair was still wet and her body was wrapped in a towel. She began to get lost deep in her thoughts, when suddenly she heard a knock at the door.

"What do you want to eat for supper?" Natalie's mother asked.

"I don't know, I'm really not hungry," she answered.

"You have to eat something. You haven't eaten in days. Jason would want you to,"

"It doesn't matter what he wants, he's not here anymore, is he?" Natalie responded before finally giving in.

She threw some clothes on and came into the kitchen. "Come over here and help me cook, that'll warm you up pretty good," her mother said, smiling.

Natalie followed her instructions and went over to her mother, who was standing over a large pot of vegetable soup on the stove. She helped cook, trying to keep herself occupied. The more she did, the more she thought about Jason. No matter what she tried, nothing took away the void."I wish I was able to cook for him like this," she thought as she stood and looked out the kitchen window, watching it snow. Her father opened up the back door, coming in the house from being outside all day. The cat heard him come in and ran over to him. He sat down at the kitchen table, and took off his shoes silently, before getting up and going to the back of the house to change. Things were different, and Natalie knew that something was off with him. After a few minutes of silence, her Father finally spoke up.

"I've been saved," he said, with tears in his eyes as he stepped back into the kitchen.

Natalie's mother ran over to him in excitement. It came as a huge surprise to everyone. They had been waiting and praying for that to happen for years.

Out of excitement, Natalie took her phone out of her pocket and out of habit, started to text Jason. Halfway through typing the message she stopped, realizing that she couldn't text him anymore. Her heart stopped as her happiness turned into sadness. "What am I doing? I'm such an idiot," She thought. She put her phone back in her pocket. Natalie tookTaking a deep breath, she placed her hand on her chest, feeling her heart pound. "He's gone," she mumbled as she fell to the floor in tears. She tried to control herself. "Get it together Natalie," she told herself.

She stood up, holding on to the wall for support as she threw her phone onto her bed from the hallway. She dried her eyes and went to the bathroom, looking at herself in the mirror. "What have I done that has caused me to be in this predicament?" She asked out loud, looking at her reflection. She washed her face and calmed down, before finally getting the courage to come back where everyone was.

"What's wrong Natalie?" Her mother asked.

"I tried to text Jason and I realized I couldn't," Natalie responded, as her voice began to crack. More tears to flow down her cheeks like rivers as she hid her face.

"Text him anyway," her mother responded, trying to make her feel better.

"What's the point? It's not like he can reply back," Natalie said, in a bitter tone of voice.

 Natalie sat down at the dining room table once she was calm, taking a few moments alone to collect herself. She looked down at her feet on the floor, trying to ignore everyone. "I can't let them see me like this," she thought, motivating herself to start eating. Hiding her emotions from those who were around her was easier than trying to explain how she actually felt. Putting her thoughts into words were impossible, and no one around her understood the way she felt.

Natalie finished and got up from the table. "I'm going to go to my room for a while" Natalie stated. Her parents nodded and she left the room. She laid down on the bed, when a thought popped into her head "Why can God save my father and not Jason?" She thought, as her body tensed up with anger.

"Lord, how could you do something like this to me after all the years I've been faithful to you?" She asked, starting to cry. It was at that moment Natalie came to the harsh realization that God did not come through for her. Her prayers were ignored. No matter how hard she prayed or how much faith she had, God still turned his back on her and he let Jason die. "Why should I continue to worship you if you're not going to protect me or the ones I love?" she asked, sobbing uncontrollably "All the Faith I had and I have nothing to show for it. I don't know why I even wasted my time following these lies," she thought, feeling like she been left out and abandoned by her God.

Natalie spent the next few hours trying to figure out why God had turned his hand away from her. She went from questioning how real God was, to wondering what sin she committed to bring punishment like this. She felt like God hated her. "Lord what have I done to you that has caused you to turn against me like this?" Natalie sat up in bed and stared up at the ceiling, taking deep breaths "Why God? Why me?" she said, with her voice cracking.

Natalie's focus quickly turned to all the bad things that happened to her throughout her life. Natalie's life had not been an easy one. It just seemed to be one disappointment after another. Nothing ever went in her favor and in the rare times that it did, something would cause it to go wrong. "Lord, I wasn't even born normal. Why did you save my life at birth to live a life this miserable?" she asked, turning her focus from the ceiling to the scar on her chest left from her heart condition.

"I can have both of my major arteries cut off and sown back on, but Jason couldn't survive a car accident," she thought. Natalie began to tremble. She couldn't go on anymore. She began to get sleepy, but fought the urge to go to sleep in fear of a dream of Jason. She laid back down, and kept thinking. "I've had to live my life with a heart condition, and so many other things. God the least you could've done for me was give me a husband!" She cried, laying her head down on the pillow, finally drifting off to sleep.

The next morning, Natalie heard a knock at her bedroom door.

"Who is it?" She mumbled, still half asleep.

"It's me," her mother said, trying to be funny.

Natalie turned over and rubbed her eyes. She groaned and sat up in bed. Stretching, she reached over to the nightstand and checked her phone. She sighed, "I forgot today was Sunday," she thought. She laid back down in the bed and nearly fell back to sleep, when the knocking on her bedroom door returned.

"What is it now?" Natalie asked, in anger. The door slowly creaked open and her mother poked her head inside.

"Do you want to go to church this morning?" She asked.

"No, not really. I told you I don't want anything to do with God anymore," Natalie said, laying in bed facing the wall.

"Come on, I think you need to,"

"Fine!,"

She gave in to her parents begging and decided to go to church. Natalie did not want to go. Just the thoughts of being at that place bothered her. She chose to go because her parents wanted her to and hopefully they would leave her alone. Natalie grumbled as she got out of bed and went into the living room, convincing herself that getting out of the house seemed like a good idea. "Maybe it won't be so bad. It's only an hour anyway," she thought, giving herself a pep talk. She sat down on the couch, put her head in her hand and struggled to wake up. Her cat jumped up on the couch and rubbed his head on her arm. She petted his head and looked at her father who was sitting in the recliner across the room from her.

"Do I really have to go?" Natalie asked, almost changing her mind.

"I think it would be good for you if you did. You'd be getting out of the house, and you can't just lay down and give up life. Plus church is one of the best places you can go," Her father responded, smiling, hoping that church would bring some comfort to her.

Natalie threw her head back against the couch, knowing she was being forced to go somewhere she didn't want to go and there was no getting out of it. She plundered through her drawers and looked for a pair of jeans to put on, wearing a skirt or a dress was out of the question. She saw a red sweater hanging in her closet. It was the first thing she saw, so she put it on. She contemplated putting makeup on, but she didn't feel like it. "Who do I have to look good for now anyway?" She thought. She brushed her hair enough so that it wasn't a long, tangled copper mess and left her room.

Natalie got her coat that was hanging on the coat rack, sat down in a kitchen chair that was near the door and waited for both her parents and her younger sister to get ready. She laid her head down on the kitchen table, dreading the next couple hours. Finally, her father came into the room and they went into the cold January air. Natalie got in the back seat, of the car and didn't say much on the ride to town. She sat and enjoyed the solitude, until Kelcie started making conversation with her and their mother.

"Mom, what do you think will happen to me if I don't go back to work?" Natalie asked, not wanting to continue on.

"Don't worry about stuff like that right now, all you need to focus on is yourself. I do think you need to work though, it will help you keep your mind off him," she replied.

"I don't know how to, though. I'm used to having him around me all the time when I worked and now he's gone," Natalie said in despair, as she laid back in the car seat, staring out the window with a blank expression. "I want to move forward. I don't want to be alone for the rest of my life and I definitely don't want to continue working, at least for right now. I'm just so confused," Natalie added.

"Just take some time off right now. I think everyone expects you to anyway. Have you told your contractors about what happened? You have to let them know,"

"Yes, I have,"she replied.

    Natalie thought about taking two months off of work. Her contractor told her to take as many days as she needed, so she took advantage of the opportunity to give her time to think about her career decision.

    Natalie's heart sank, as the car pulled into the church parking lot. Memories of Jason's funeral resurfaced in her mind as the car came to a stop. "I don't want to be here," she griped. As she got out of the car, her phone vibrated. She was shaking so bad that getting her phone out of her pocket was a challenge. She finally got a solid grip around it and checked the notification. "Oh it's Blake," she thought, cheering her up a little bit, as she read the message.

"Can we meet up to talk sometime soon?"

"Yeah, we can," Natalie replied quickly putting her phone away.

    Natalie stood and stared at the bright red church. She was nervous about going inside. She was mad at God to begin with, so she didn't want to be there. As she walked to the door, the gravel crunching under each step, she regretted that she didn't fight harder to stay home. "I don't think I can do this!" Natalie said, stopping dead in her tracks at the entrance.

"You'll be alright," her mother comforted her. She stood there for a while before finally mustering up the courage to go through the doors.

Natalie burst into tears and her parents rushed over to help her. They each grabbed one of Natalie's arms, helping her walk through the vestibule. Natalie went silent after stepping through the door. Everyone's eyes were on her, and she knew it. She sat down in a pew next to a stained glass window in the far right corner of the church, trying to isolate herself from the crowd as much as possible. She did not want to be there, she did not want attention. The only thing she wanted was her life back.

Natalie burst into tears and her parents rushed over to help her. They each grabbed one of Natalie's arms, helping her walk through the vestibule. She went silent after stepping into the sanctuary. Everyone was staring at her. She sat down in a pew, next to a stained glass window, in the far right corner of the church trying to isolate herself from the crowd as much as possible. She hated attention, she just wanted her life back.

The musicians came from the back to the altar. "I'd like to dedicate this song to my good buddy, Jason Tackett," the singer said as the band began to play a song out of the hymnal. Natalie's heart stopped and tears rolled down her face. The noise of people singing aggravated her.

The song ended after what felt like an eternity. She had some peace, until she realized it was time for fellowship. People from all over the building came up to her, hugging her and telling her that everything was going to be okay. The pastor noticed she was crying and came over to pray for her. Jason's cousin came up to Natalie and hugged her with tears in her eyes. That was enough to push Natalie over the edge and she broke down.

The service came to an end. It only lasted an hour, but to Natalie it felt like fifty years. She slowly made her way out to the vestibule where the rest of her family was at, feeling relief that this was over. The pastor had pulled her father to the side and she noticed them talking.

"That's one of the strongest things I've ever seen," the pastor said, bragging on her. Natalie's father shook his hand while she stepped outside to get some fresh air and relax. Her father was to meet back with the pastor the next day to discuss his baptism.

    Natalie came home from church feeling like life had been drained out of her. She barely made it through the back door before dropping her purse on the kitchen floor. "I'll pick it up later," she thought, as she headed towards her bedroom where peace and quiet awaited her. She had a pounding headache from stress. She opened her bedroom door and went straight to the vanity to change clothes, fully intending on taking a nap. She sat down and stared at herself in the vanity mirror. She rubbed her forehead trying to ease her headache. She stood up from the vanity, picked up some blue shorts and a white t-shirt and put them on.

Natalie finally felt relaxed. For a few moments, she was happy. Happy to be alone and by herself. Natalie sat down on her bed, and put her hair up. She reclined her legs and just sat there, enjoying the silence. She took a few deep breaths, "thank God that's over," she thought, being genuinely grateful for having conquered something so difficult.

After a little bit of peace, Natalie's eyelids got heavy. "I'm not gonna let myself go to sleep today," she told herself in an attempt to fight the urge she had to sleep.

Her mind drifted once again to how bad her life had been. Specifically, her experience in school from grade school to high school, she was always different than the other kids. She was covered in freckles and very pale skinned. She tried to fit it, but she couldn't no matter how hard she tried. Everything that Natalie tried to do never seemed to work out in her favor, even in adulthood.

The very next morning, a brand new week had began. Natalie laid awake in bed, staring the ceiling, "How did I make it this far with out him?" She thought. She forced herself to get out of bed, groaning with every move she made. Natalie slowly rose up, pulling the cover off of her legs. She stretched and looked at her phone on the was charging on the nightstand next to her. Unaware that she was looking to see if Jason had texted her. She cried and turned her off. Leaving it alone. It had been over a week since Natalie had gotten to see Jason, and that was really tough for her. Neither Natalie or Jason we're apart from each other for more than two days. "This is wrong." Natalie said, sobbing. simply didn't feel right, knowing that he was supposed to be here and he wasn't here. Trying to adjust was both difficult and painful.

Chapter 3

The bright morning sun was peeking through the blinds. Natalie scratched her eyes, it was Sunday morning. "Oh no," Natalie thought as she sat up in the bed. She rubbed her forehead, dreading the day ahead. She knew she had to face it, whether she wanted to or not. Her feet hit the warm gray carpet in her bedroom, as she went into the living room. Today was the day of her father's baptism.

That evening, she was going to meet up with Jason's best friend Blake. Natalie was so nervous that her insides quivered. She didn't know him very well. She only knew a little bit about him from the few times that he visited with Jason and stories that she had heard about him. He felt like more of a stranger than a friend. Both of them wanted to support each other. He lost a brother and she lost a husband. Natalie was the only one around Blake who could understand his pain, and he could understand hers.

The day seemed to go on forever. Evening couldn't come fast enough. She was excited to finally be able to talk to someone outside of her family.

As five o'clock drew closer, she began to get nervous. "This will be good for me," she told herself, trying to calm down. She got up from the couch and sat down to put makeup on. She didn't feel like putting very much on, so she used just enough concealer and foundation to hide the dark circles under her eyes.

This was the first time she had been out in public, other than church, since Jason died and Natalie was worried about what others would say. Not just being out with his best friend. She took a deep breath and tried to calm her mind as much as possible. She grabbed her cream colored sweater from the coat rack hanging on the back of her bedroom door. "I'm really overthinking this," she thought, as she made her way into the kitchen and waited for him to arrive. "I should be waiting on Jason to come pick me up," she thought as she sat in the wooden chair at the kitchen table.

She sighed as she thought about Jason. She texted her mother and told her what was going on, explaining to her that she wouldn't be home that evening. A little while later, Blake finally pulled into the driveway in a pickup truck that Natalie didn't recognize. He opened the door and was cleaning a seat out for her.

"Hi, how have you been holding up?" Blake asked.

"Well, today's been a little bit of a better day," Natalie replied, as she got into the black pickup truck.

"Yeah, that's me. It's not been so bad for me either," he said, getting in the drivers seat.

Natalie felt a little odd and out of place. She didn't know what to say, or what to do. She was shy and struggled communicating with others she didn't know too well.

"I don't know what's wrong with the radio, it keeps playing 80's music," Blake said, laughing.

"It's okay,"

She was silent most of the way to town. They decided to eat at a local Mexican restaurant before he came and picked Natalie up. When they got there, Natalie's heart sank. She got her purse and got out of the truck, adjusting her shirt tail out of nervousness. "What is he going to think about me? Better yet, what is he going to tell me?" she thought as she walked in the door behind him.

They waited for a few moments on a table and sat down. "This isn't the same," Natalie said to Blake, sitting on the opposite side of the table.

"I know it's not," he said.

Natalie felt her eyes getting wet and her face warm. Trying to hide the tears, she changed the subject and talked about the weather. The conversation quickly came back to what happened to Jason.

"I hate that boy so much," Natalie said.

"He's my cousin, and I hate him too," Blake responded.

Natalie could no longer hold back her tears. She cried quietly, and Blake did too. He missed Jason as much as she did. She took a deep breath, wiped her eyes and then laughed at the embarrassment of crying in public. She mustered up the courage to ask a very important question.

"Blake, did they send the truck to be investigated?" Natalie asked.

"Jason's mom asked me the exact same thing. They were supposed to, but that's all I know," Blake responded.

Natalie breathed a sigh of relief upon hearing that news, "Thank God, because I don't believe that there was a mechanical failure,"

"I don't either. Mechanical failures don't leave black marks seventy five feet on the road," Blake responded.

Natalie's stomach turned, realizing that it wasn't an accident. She pushed her food away. "Are you okay?" Blake asked.

"Yeah, I'm okay. I just can't eat when I think or talk about this," Natalie replied forcing herself to hold back tears.

"I feel ya! Though sometimes I do the opposite and eat more than I should," he responded.

"I miss that man so much,"

"I know, I do too," Blake responded.

"You know, I blame myself for this happening and I'm really struggling with that," she said.

"He wanted to spend time with me all day and I didn't. Don't think I haven't regretted that,"

The two of them finished up their evening and left the restaurant. On their way home it began to snow. Natalie got excited at the snow, but thought about Jason and how much he loved it. He always wanted enough snow to cancel school, so he didn't have to go to work.

Natalie returned home that night at nine. She came through the door and threw her purse down on the kitchen table and immediately went to go change clothes. She wished that things were different. Life without Jason was dull and meaningless. After changing into some pajamas, she went back to sit with her parents.

"Did you have a good time?" Her father asked.

"Yeah, it was okay. I learned a lot of things I didn't know," Natalie responded.

"What did he know?" Her mother asked.

"Not much more than I did, other than the fact that Dustin was drunk. I also learned that they won't release the 911 tapes," Natalie said.

"Of course he was drunk, a blind man could've seen that," Kelcie chimed in.

"Why won't they release the 911 tapes? Isn't that illegal?" Her father asked.

"I have no idea, but it's suspicious," Natalie said.

She talked with her family for a little while and took some time to process everything Blake told her. She already had an idea of what he was going to tell her, but actually hearing it was different. Her worst fears were confirmed right there in a matter of minutes.

Natalie looked at the clock and decided to go to bed, realizing it was way past eleven. She forced herself to get up off the couch, and went to her room to get ready for bed. When her feet hit the gray carpet in her bedroom, she felt her phone buzz. "It's probably nothing," she thought and threw her phone down on the bed. She sat down at her vanity and looked at herself in the mirror. "Have I looked like this all evening?" She questioned, looking at her melted makeup and dark circles. She reached for some cotton balls soaked with makeup remover. The coolness of the damp cotton ball against her face was calming and oddly relaxing. Natalie finished, closing the lid to her acrylic jar. She got up and stretched, feeling good and relaxed for the first time in a really long time.

Natalie set her clock for ten the next morning, trying to get some kind of normal routine started. She climbed into bed, her cat jumped up and curled up on top of her feet. She looked at him and smiled and picked up her phone. Her heart stopped when she saw she had a message from her ex Zeke. "Why God? I actually felt good today," she said out loud as she read the message.

"Would you ever let me become your boyfriend again?" The message said.

"Never," Natalie responded and tried to ignore the rest of his messages. She rolled over in bed and sighed in frustration. Knowing that Zeke was only going to get worse from here. He was terrible to her and no matter what she did, he would never leave her alone.

She turned back over on her back and noticed Jason's prayer shawl that she stored away on her bookshelf. She got up out of bed and went to pick up the blue velvet pouch it was in. She opened it and held the blue and white shawl in her hands. "I miss him so much," she thought as she pressed the shawl up against her chest. It still smelled like his cologne, making her miss him more. "This is all I have left of him," she thought as she began to cry.

"How could you do this to me God?" Natalie asked, as she collapsed into tears. She started thinking about what she could have had if Jason made it. "What have I done wrong?" She asked, thinking of every sin she committed. Nothing made sense. There was no way to explain why things happened the way they did.

Natalie took a few deep breaths and pulled herself together. She put away those things and left the room for a few minutes to clear her mind. In the bathroom was some anxiety medication. She wanted to hold off on taking the medicine for as long as she could, but caved after the anxiety became too much to bare. She felt wrong for taking the medicine. A church friend of hers, who was helping her through her healing journey, told her that medication was a sin and our joy comes from the Lord. Natalie's Joy in the Lord was no longer there, because God did not come through for her. She stopped thinking and the medicine kicked in. She climbed back into bed and relaxed, doing some breathing exercises that helped her calm down.

Natalie completely relaxed and finally got sleepy. She turned the lights off and turned the television on, for some background noise as she slept. Natalie watched an old sitcom on tv and began to slowly close her eyes. The cool air blowing from the fan kept her comfortable and the warmth of her bed encased her. She went to sleep, dreaming about Jason and the life that they were supposed to have.

Chapter 4

Natalie's long journey of healing had begun, but there was still a very long way to go. Everyday was a struggle. She thought about Jason constantly, never being able to get him out of her mind. There were days when she'd have tell herself to stop thinking about him. Though it was considered unhealthy, she found comfort in it.

Natalie reflected a lot on her relationship with Jason. She examined every part of it. From the things she did wrong to the things she did right. She missed him so bad, that it physically hurt, but she was slowly becoming aware of the fact that no matter how much she thought about him, he wasn't coming back.

One morning, A horrible fear took over Natalie. A part of her had been taken away, but was worried she would never find anyone else again. Her chest tightened and her heart skipped a few beats. It was a very real possibility that she'd never meet anyone again. Natalie had a desire to move forward. She knew she wanted to, but didn't know where to begin. "I'm too broken for anyone to ever love me," she thought, letting herself get discouraged

Her thoughts were running her life. Her mind was in turmoil and she found it hard to distinguish between reality and fiction. "I don't think I'm ever going to heal from this. Why would you want to? Is it even worth it? because there's no point in continuing," she said, expressing her emotions to her church pastor, sitting in his office.

The pastor looked at her with his eyes filled with sorrow. "I don't know why the Lord chose to make his life so short. I do know that whatever he takes away, he always gives something back in return. Like Job for example," he said, starting to cry with Natalie.

The pastor handed her a piece of candy and told her to eat. She declined the offer, and got up to leave. Natalie came home, and finally had some time to herself. She sighed a sigh of relief as she sat down on the couch. She laid her head back against the cushion and her mind began to wander.

Natalie had no one to lean on for support. She felt alone. Her parents had gone back to work, and she was left at home by herself. All she had was her cat. Natalie became severely depressed, since the shock of what happened wore off. She began to think of suicide, wanting to overdose on sleep medication. Killing herself was her only option to get rid of all the pain and despair. She rose up and shook her head. "Oh my God, what am

I doing?" She thought, that she actually planned on taking her own life.

The things Natalie used to do, she no longer had interest in. She could not work, playing music was now a thing of the past and now all she did most of the day was sleep. Sleeping was Natalie's favorite thing to do, because it was the only way she could escape the pain and forget about reality.

That afternoon, Natalie woke up from a very deep sleep. She stretched and didn't realize she had fallen asleep. She rolled over and made herself comfortable there on the couch, underneath the warmth of the blanket on top of her. She looked up at the ceiling, yawned and stretched, finally throwing the covers off and getting up. The sleepiness cleared, as she sat up and turned on the news. Her heart broke as a story came on about someone else being killed in a car wreck.

"I can relate," she thought as her heart began to pound. She quickly turned the television back off, as feelings of guilt began to resurface from flashbacks of the night Jason died. She remembered it too well.

Natalie was at Jason's house, sitting on his couch by the living room window. It was almost eleven o'clock at night. She was tired from wedding dress shopping, and she knew it was time to go home.

"It won't be much longer until you never have to go back home," Jason said, looking at Natalie, smiling.

Natalie put her black boots on to go outside and start her car. " I know and I'm looking forward to it," Natalie said, zipping her boots and getting up off the couch. She opened his seventies style front door and stepped out on to the cold front porch. She ran across the frozen grass in the yard with her arms wrapped around her. "It's so cold," she thought as she opened her car door and fell into the seat. She stuck the key into the ignition and started her car. The temperature read four degrees.

She got out of the car and left it running, hoping that it would melt the solid sheet of ice off of her windshield. She went back inside the house to wait.
"Oh you're back so fast," Jason joked.

Natalie laughed and took her coat off. Jason was playing video games, and enjoying himself and not wanting to interrupt, she played with their dog Charles. She stopped for a moment. Something just seemed off about the evening.
"What's the matter?" Jason asked, looking at the concern on Natalie's face.
"Oh, Nothing. Things just feel a little weird," Natalie said, not knowing how to put what she was feeling into words.

Natalie sat around and waited for about ten minutes and then decided it was time to go.

"You're leaving already?" Jason asked, as Natalie stood up.

"I have to, it's really late,"

"I can't wait until this is your home," he said, gazing at Natalie with a loving look on his face.

Jason got up and kissed her. They said their goodbyes and she went back outside to find that her car had wasn't running. Confused, she started it again. It was cold natured, and was known of not being able to start in weather under thirty degrees. Still she had no luck.

Natalie knee that it took jumper cables to get her cold nature car started. She got back out of the car, frustrated, and went back inside the house.

"You're back!" Jason said, surprised.

"Yeah, my car is being stupid. Can you jump my car?" She asked. Jason looked up at her and said "Don't worry about that, I'll take you home instead. Just let me change my clothes," he said, still in his pajamas.

Natalie stood by the door, with her purse in hand, and waited on him to change.

"Okay, I'm ready," he said, as he came back into the living room and grabbed his keys from the key rack behind Natalie.

Jason opened the door, and followed Natalie outside, taking the dog with them. On the way to her house, they discussed their wedding plans. Jason was just as excited as Natalie was.

Natalie shook her head, coming back into reality. With her heart still racing, she thought about how often he told he dreamed of having a family. Even as a child, his desire was always to get married and start a family. Little did they know, that night would be the last time Natalie would ever see him again and both of their dreams were cut short.

Natalie started to tear up and became overwhelmed with guilt. "If only my car had started. Why wouldn't he just let me use the jumper cables?" she thought, rubbing her forehead. She tried not to think about it, but the guilt was overtaking her. "He never got to live his dream," she thought, blaming herself for his death and not marrying him immediately after proposal.

She begged God for a way to go back in time and change things. Jason begged her to run off and get married, but she didn't want to because she always dreamed of having a large church wedding. "I just had to have a wedding, didn't I," she thought, feeling selfish for making him wait and wondering if it would have saved his life.

Natalie laid her head back against the couch and began to wonder if she was there for him enough. She loved him and worried about whether she showed it to him enough. "I could have supported him more," she thought, staring at the living room ceiling.

Natalie regretted not being there for him as much as she could have been. He struggled so much with his job, and his boss who was making his life miserable. He would come home from work every evening upset and frustrated because he felt like he was being singled out. She tried to comfort him as much as she could, but it never worked. She always felt like she wasn't doing enough.

Natalie got up and tried to clear her mind from the negative thoughts. She started cleaning and doing anything she could do to get her mind off of Jason. She cleaned everything that she could, until every room in the house was spotless.

Natalie took a deep breath and sat down on the bed to rest. "I've got to

Talk to someone about this," she thought, running her fingers through her hair. "I'm literally loosing my mind," she thought, falling back onto the bed. She picked up her phone that was buried underneath the bed pillows. "Do you mind if I talk to you about this? I'm having a really hard time," she typed, but hesitated to send the message to her church pastor, worried about opening up to him.

"Of course," he responded quickly, giving Natalie a feeling of relief.

"I feel so guilty. He'd still be here if it wasn't for my car not starting," she told Derrick.

"You can't blame yourself for something that was out of your control. It wasn't up to you whether the car started or not," he said, to reassure her that it wasn't her fault.

"I could have called my parents to come and get me," she said

"Do you honestly think Jason would have let you do that? He was taking care of the woman he loved,"

"How do I stop blaming myself then?"Natalie asked.

"You don't have to listen to those thoughts. You're a child of God and have authority over them. Cast them down in the name of Jesus," he said.

Natalie took his advice, and tried to cast down the thoughts that intruded her mind every day. It worked for a while, but took no time at all for her to start thinking about it again. Frustrated, she kept doing that when those thoughts came into her mind and making her anxious. "Satan, leave me alone," she shouted and commanded the negative thoughts to leave. Each time, they would leave for a while, but they would always come back. Often, she would just give in because it was easier than fighting it.

That night, Natalie dealt with self hatred. She felt that she was unworthy of life. There was no point in going on if she couldn't be happy. She filled up the sink full of water and washed her face. The warm water on her face relieved her tension headache. She looked up in the mirror, staring at herself, wishing her life would end. She no longer wanted to commit suicide, after realizing that she wasn't in control of whether she chose to live or die. Instead, she prayed each night for God to take her life away.

Natalie dried her face and looked at her reflection, hating everything that she saw. She was unhappy with how she looked. "I'm too ugly to find anyone else," she scoffed, looking at her face full of freckles. She sighed and turned the light off, knowing it was time for bed.

Chapter 5

The next morning, Natalie noticed it was February the first. "Wow, that went by so fast," she thought, sitting up in bed rubbing her head. January passed like the blink of an eye. She knew she had her first big hurdle in just two weeks. Valentine's Day. She groaned at the thought of Valentine's Day and got up out of bed. "Why do we even celebrate that for anyway?" she thought, stretching.

Things like this used to excite Natalie, now anything that had to do with love and relationships, she despised. She came into the living room and thought about how she was going to avoid it this year. She was prepared to take extreme measures to stay away from it at all costs, even if it meant staying away from certain places.

Everyone made jokes about romance being dead, but hers was literally dead. "People shouldn't joke about that," Natalie thought, spending the rest of the day trying not to think about it. "It's just another day. Besides, dreading it is probably worse than what it will actually be," she kept telling herself. She tried hard to forget about Jason. Thinking about him made it worse, but if she stopped, she felt guilty. She prayed for those memories, of her relationship with Jason, to be erased. "I wish I had never met him," she thought, slamming the utility room door.

Natalie stayed pent up in her house for the next several days. She wanted to get out, but she knew it would only hurt her if she did. She convinced that she was loosing her mind. "Is it normal to feel this way?" She questioned herself.

Feeling particularly lonely, Natalie turned to other people for help. She felt like she was stranded, because no one was there to support her. No matter how many people she reached out to, they either didn't respond or they didn't help. A few people made it worse by saying "Oh you'll find someone else," The problem was that Natalie did not want anyone else. She only wanted Jason.

At this point, she was spending most of her day in her bed, trying to avoid everything and everyone. People who weren't able to help her were ignored. Natalie fell into a very deep depression, sometimes sleeping up to eighteen hours a day. She was asleep more than she was awake. She had no energy to keep herself awake, but she enjoyed sleeping. When she was asleep, she didn't have to face reality. When she was awake, she would not leave her room or house. Everyday, all she could think of how alone she was. All of her friends abandoned her, Jason was dead and all Natalie had left was her family and a cat.

To distract herself, she spent copious amounts of time on the internet connecting with others in a support group, who had also been through similar situations. "I had everything I ever wanted and now I'm sitting here alone in a support group," Natalie thought, though she noticed it was slightly helping. That same afternoon, Natalie tried to change her routine. Forcing herself to stay awake. Out of habit, She would bring up Facebook, even though it was detrimental to her mental state. As she was scrolling through her news feed, Natalie stumbled upon photos of people who had celebrated Valentine's Day early. Hundreds of images of red roses people spending time together, and just gifts in general made her sick to her stomach and outraged with jealousy. "How come they get everything I wanted and I'm stuck here dealing with this?" Natalie whispered quietly.

The only way her body reacted was by crying. She locked her phone screen and let her emotions flow. She kept her bedroom door shut, hiding her emotions. She wanted to appear strong to others, and herself. She didn't like feeling this pain. "I have got to stop doing this to myself," she thought, vowing to herself to stay off of social media for the rest of the week. She felt bad for being jealous of others. She wanted to be happy for them, but she couldn't. They had such great lives, while hers stopped dead in its tracks.

Natalie was finally able to enjoy some peace that evening. She was resting in her bed, thinking about her future. "I wonder when I'll meet someone else," she thought, pondering the idea of meeting someone. Natalie thought about the occult, and decided to get a psychic reading. "It won't hurt, I just want to try it out," she thought, searching the web for psychics. Tarot card readings provided fast answers for her, satisfying her need for the answers that she longed for. One psychic told her not to worry, that she would meet someone new at the end of 2018. Hearing that made Natalie feel good, and eased her mind for a few days.

    Natalie took her answer and enjoyed the high that it gave her, even though she knew that meeting someone at the end of the year was unlikely. She was able to focus on other things since that worry had been taken away from her. Natalie finally felt happy and came into the dining room, where here parents were. They had opened a new jigsaw puzzle and were sitting around the table putting it together. She smiled at them, and sat down beside them.

"Well, lope decided to come in and join us," her father said, calling her by her nickname before he got up and left the room, leaving her to take over for him.

"Yeah, I did. I emerged from my cave," she chuckled.

For the first time in a long time, she was truly enjoying herself. Watching the warm fire flicker in the distance, the crackling of the wood was a soothing sound. Natalie and Kelcie created a contest, trying to see who could find the most pieces the fastest. Natalie found the piece she was looking for and slammed it into the slot, shaking the table with a loud thud.

"Natalie!" Kelcie exclaimed sarcastically. "What in the world was that?!" She asked laughing.

"I...I... don't know," Natalie said, trying to catch her breath from squealing with laughter.

"I found it first!" Natalie exclaimed.

"You all hush in there. I can't hear my tv show," Their father said, who was sitting on the couch in the opposite room from them.

Natalie laid back in her chair, smiling like things were normal again. She thought about Jason, and how he would have loved to be here with her right now.

Remembering him, she spoke up shared a memory about him with Kelcie.

"Jason used to make fun of me all the time for this," Natalie said.

"No wonder. You're the only person in the world who could screw up a puzzle," Kelcie said.

Natalie smiled once again, realizing how lucky she was to have a supportive family helping her through this. Once they were finished puzzling for the night, they went into the living room. Natalie relaxed in the recliner and zoned out, reminiscing the not so distant past.

The clock struck midnight, bringing her back to reality from being in her thoughts. "Oh no, it's here," she thought as she got up out of the floor and walked to her bedroom to retire for the night. Natalie quietly went into her room, and flopped down on the bed, wanting nothing more than to just be left alone tomorrow. She sighed and looked up at the ceiling, "I'm gonna have to do this aren't I?" She questioned, but Natalie's grandmother insisted that she go out and do something with her on Valentine's Day. Her grandmother wanted her to feel better, and Natalie agreed. There was nothing to make her feel better, but she chose to go to make her grandmother feel like she was making a difference. She also felt bad about turning away her own grandmother and her father wasn't giving her an option. Natalie's mind quickly came to thinking about sleep. She wasn't going to get to sleep in."Why does my family do everything at the crack of dawn?" She whined, before closing her eyes.

Ten o'clock in the morning came fast. Her father came into Natalie's bedroom and kicked the bed. "Oh my God, don't do that to me," she screamed. She got up, still sleepy from staying awake so late and now she was angry. She headed straight to the bathroom, looked at herself in the mirror and saw the dark circles underneath her eyes. She touched them, rubbing them as if that was going to make them disappear. They were darker than normal, a deep purple shade that made her face look bruised. She turned the sink on and washed her face, preparing it to put on makeup for the first time in over a month. She raised her face up from the sink, drying it on a freshly washed pink towel, and made her way back to her bedroom. She got her makeup compact out of her vanity drawer. She opened it and the perfumed smell hit her nose. Her heart stopped. "I can't wear this foundation, the smell reminds me too much of Jason," she thought, putting it back in the drawer.

At that point, she wanted to go back to bed and just give up, but her father encouraged her to go. Natalie frantically rummaged through her vanity drawers and found something to go on her face that wasn't scented and roughly covered up her dark circles. She put on some mascara, lip gloss and soft flesh colored eyeshadow, so she didn't look like she hadn't slept in years. Natalie laid back against her bright green bedroom walls, took a deep breath, and powered through the sleepiness and pain. "It might be fun," she thought, trying to motivate herself.

Natalie came into the kitchen, carrying her bright pink converse tennis shoes. She sat down in a kitchen chair and waited for her grandmother to arrive, tying her shoes. "Where's my coat?" She asked her father.

"I don't know," he answered.

"Gosh you're so much help," she said, bitterly because she had to go.

Suddenly, she pulled up to the house in her bright blue SUV, a few minutes early, as usual. "Hurry up Kelcie, mamaw's here!" Natalie screamed. Kelcie came running into the kitchen, and grabbed her purse. Natalie was looking for her jacket when she heard her blow the car horn. Only two minutes later, she blew the horn again. "Oh my Lord, she can't wait five minutes can she?" she asked, aggravated that she was being rushed. Natalie finally found her jacket hanging in the utility room and she put it on, walking out the door. Once again, she heard the car horn.

"I'm coming Mamaw!" she said out loud in the house to herself.

"Your mother is impatient," Kelcie told her father, jokingly who was standing with his back up against the stove. She got her things together and went outside with her sister Kelcie.

"We gotta hurry" Kelcie said, as they walked down the back porch steps in the bitter cold air.

Natalie got in the front seat of the car and Kelcie in the back.

"Natalie, didn't you want to wear makeup today?" Her grandmother asked.

"Not really. I basically put on enough to cover the tiredness on my face," she responded.

Deciding where to eat was always a challenge for Natalie. Making decisions was never easy for her and gave her anxiety. She let her sister choose where to eat and from there they went shopping at local businesses.

Natalie came home that night exhausted and thankful to be home. She kicked her shoes off and sat down in the recliner, pulling her hair up with a hair tie that was on the end table next to her. To her surprise, getting out of the house made her feel better. Seeing new faces in new places made her forget about the pain she felt, even for just a little while.

Chapter 6

Natalie was resting at home, one dark and cold February morning. The events of the previous week left her exhausted both mentally and physically. "I'm not going anywhere with anyone this week," she thought, as she reclined out on the couch. It was the end of the month and she was looking forward to March. Spring has always been one of her favorite times of the year. The winter months were depressing and this winter was worse than most. Months of snow and ice were taking its toll on her mental health. That morning, the sun was slightly brighter and it was unusually warm. It gave her hope.

Natalie got up and stood in her kitchen looking out the window at the spring like day, sipping on a glass of tea. "It's such a beautiful day," she thought as she smiled. For the first time since the accident, Natalie felt like she was going to make it through this. She stepped outside and took a deep breath, taking in and enjoying the warmer air. Her mood improved, as she stared at the bare trees in the distance.

Suddenly, she heard the door open behind her. It startled her. She jumped and placed her hand on her chest, feeling her fluttering heart. "Don't sneak up on me like that!" She squealed, turning around to see her father standing and laughing at her so hard that he couldn't catch his breath.

"It's not that funny," Natalie said, laughing.

"Yeah it is," her father said.

"Hey, you wanna go up behind the barn with me? It's too pretty of a day to stay stuck inside," her father asked.

"Yeah I guess, I'm not turning down an opportunity to go pet the animals,"

Natalie quickly went back inside and changed into a flannel shirt and a pair of jeans. She came back outside and got on their ATV that her father drove to the barn in front of her grandmother's old house. Feeling the wind through her hair once again reminded her of Jason, and her mind quickly went to thinking about him. "I wonder if he'd be doing this with me today?" She pondered. She missed him so much. Everything she did reminded her of Jason, and she couldn't stop thinking about how he would have liked to be there for these things. There was a hole inside Natalie's soul that was too big to fill.

As the day went on, she spent most of her time outside watching the world go by and just enjoyed nature. Natalie smiled and actually enjoyed the difference of the day. "This is my new life, at least for now anyway," she thought, finally accepting the reality of what had happened to her.

Later that week, the cold and nasty weather returned. One day in particular, it was raining hard. The sky was dark and Natalie was hit with a wave of emotional distress. Her depression was at its worst as she struggled to get out of the bed to do anything. "Why don't you just kill yourself?" She thought. "It'd be much easier than living through this pain," Natalie pushed her dark thoughts to the side, trying to hide them from the people around her.

"Did you sleep good last night?" Her mother asked as she stepped into the hallway.

"Yeah, I did. I think I'm starting to get back on a normal sleep schedule," Natalie responded, being truthful, but she couldn't shake her suicidal thoughts. All day, she thought about how much better off she would be dead. There were more positives to death than negative at this point. It seemed stupid to live the rest of her life in this much pain, when it could all go away easily and she'd never go through something like this again. Natalie shook her head, realizing that these thoughts were not normal.

No matter how much she fought, she continued to slip into a deeper depression. People around her kept accidentally reminding her of Jason's death. That same evening, Natalie ventured into the living room. She was feeling decent. Suicide was not her focus for once. Her mother was talking on the phone, when she overheard a conversation that made Natalie stop dead in her tracks.

"I often wonder what Jason's last thoughts were,"

"I really did not need to hear that," Natalie interrupted.

"That wasn't what I meant, I was talking…"

"I get it, but I don't need to hear things like that. Don't talk about it when I'm around," Natalie said in a sharp tone

Natalie ran out of the room and flopped down on her bed. "I need to get out of this house, or I'm going to loose my mind," she thought, as she laid and couldn't help but wonder what Jason's last thoughts were. "Was he thinking about me?" She questioned, as she remembered the amount of pain he was in before he died. "He probably wasn't thinking about anything but the pain," she thought. Natalie sat up and forced herself to stop thinking about that. She ran her fingers through her hair when suddenly she heard a knock at the door. "Do you wanna go to the store with me?" Her mother asked.

"Yeah I guess," Natalie agreed, knowing that getting out of the house would do wonders for her. She jumped up off the bed and changed into some actual clothes instead of pajamas. Just wearing a pair of jeans and a shirt made her feel a little better. She came back into the living room to get her jacket and put her shoes on. "I'm ready to go," she told her mother, as she walked out the door and got in the car. It was just the two of them together for the first time in a while.

The grocery store parking lot was completely full. The size of the crowd was overwhelming and made Natalie question her decision of whether coming to the store was a good idea.

"Oh my God, are they giving things away? I've never seen this place so crowded," Natalie said, making a joke to try dealing with the stress in the situation.

"They must be," her mother responded.

Inside the store, she saw some familiar faces. "Oh no," she thought, as she done everything she could to dodge them. "I do not need to hear how sorry they are about my loss today,"

Natalie went her own way, avoiding them like the plague as she went through aisles. Natalie was surprised at how well she was doing. She was hid from the people she knew, and just walking around outside the house felt good.

Unexpectedly, in the large crowds of people, An older woman, who knew Natalie and her family, saw her inside the store and approached her. "Oh no, here we go,"she sighed as the woman placed her shopping cart right in front of theirs to get their attention. "Well, hello! How are you doing honey?" The woman asked Natalie.

"I'm doing okay. As good as someone who's in my situation can do," She responded, biting her lip to keep from saying anything else. She hated people asking her questions. It just reminded her of the trauma.

"I hate to hear about what happened to you. It's so awful," the old woman muttered, pausing for a moment. "Is it true that he was still alive and was the one who dialed 911?" She asked with hesitation, looking at Natalie straight in the eyes.

Natalie gave her a sharp glance, as she stood there trying to wrap her head around what her ears just heard. "Why would you want to know something like that?" Natalie asked, in a harsh tone feeling her stomach in her throat and trying to keep it together.

"I heard someone say that, the other day, and you know how rumors are. I wanted to know what the truth was and I knew you'd be the one to know that,"

Natalie took a deep breath and responded "Listen… he was unconscious when I got there and from, what I was told, he became unconscious around the time of impact. I have no idea who called the ambulance, but what I do know that's a question I never want an answer to," Natalie responded, leaving the cart and storming off.

She found her mother over by the produce, putting some tomatoes in a bag. "We have to get out of here," Natalie said explaining what had just happened to her.

They got what few things they needed, and Natalie ran out of the store in the freezing cold rain, to the car, leaving her mother to pay for the groceries. She got inside, slammed the door shut and broke down.

She wanted to give up. No matter how hard she tried to avoid people, they still somehow managed to find her. "They don't care about me, they only care about the rumors. I'm so sick of people making stuff up," she screamed. Her mental state was quickly deteriorating. She hated everything and everyone. "Why do they always bother me? Is it really that hard to leave someone alone?" She asked, looking up at the car's ceiling through her tears. "It never fails, they always ask me on days when I feel better," She thought, continuing to sob.

Natalie through her head back against the car seat in frustration and stared at the ceiling, breathing deeply to calm herself down. Ten minutes passed and she came back to reality, but it felt like an eternity. Her mother was putting the groceries in the trunk. She ran her cold hands through her red hair, pushing the wet strands out of her face. She rubbed her eyes and wrapped her arms around herself, trying to keep warm. She started the car and got out, offering to help. Her mother refused, and she got back inside the car. It was cold day. At only thirty degrees outside she was freezing from just being out for a few moments. She noticed the radio was on and Jason's favorite song started playing. Hearing the lyrics upset her deeply. "Why this of all things?" She questioned. She turned the radio off, forcefully. "I can't deal with this today,"

Natalie and her mother finally left the store and took the long way home due to all the heavy rain. She turned the radio back on, but to a different station, and focused on the music as she rode in the passengers seat down the curvy country road. She didn't talk much on the way home, creating an awkward silence in the car. Natalie was tired, emotionally and physically. The sky was pitch black, and there were no street lights. Only the headlights of the car and the glow from lights on in nearby homes. The darkness made her uncomfortable. She never liked taking that road home at night, but it was a better option than the road where Jason was killed.

Natalie was relieved to be on her way home. Being the introvert she is, having time away from people was blissful. Communicating with people was very difficult for her and gave her terrible anxiety. Now, all of a sudden, she was the center of attention. Everywhere she went, people stared or asked questions about what happened. The only place she truly felt comfortable was home.

Like a double edged sword, if she stayed at home too much, Her feelings of hopelessness and depression would take over. It was either one extreme or the other, no in between.

Once she arrived home, The depression was taking over her life and she couldn't deal with it anymore. Every day, thoughts of suicide plagued her mind, and was driving her insane. "I can't tell anyone about this, because if I do they'll think I'm crazy," she thought, frustrated at not being able to express how she truly felt. She kept her suicidal thoughts to herself, not knowing what else to do with them.

She knew that she couldn't take her own life. Natalie didn't want to pass to her family the same trauma that she went through. "I'm really gonna have to do something about this. I can't live this miserable," she thought, pondering all the possibilities and options that were available. "What am I going to do?" she questioned. She went to her room and sat down and her desk, opening the blinds to look out the window. "I can't turn to God, he didn't even help me in the first place, if he would have, my life would be totally different," she thought, quickly snapped back into reality

    Natalie Choose to turn away from God completely. It was easier for her to take matters into her own hands and lean on herself for healing. Natalie got to the point where she couldn't take the pain anymore. She was losing her mind, so she made the decision to go see a therapist. "I need this. I really need this," she told herself. She was not too worried about what people would say about her, though she knew people would make rude comments and call her crazy. There was a terrible stigma in Eastern Kentucky. If you went to see a therapist, you were immediately deemed by the public as senile. Natalie knew she had nothing to lose and she put her fears of what the public would say to the side. She didn't care anymore about what people thought, she just knew she needed help and was thankful that she was able to realize that before it was too late. "It's not too late is it?" She asked as she picked up the house phone, and called the number that a close friend of her family had given her and made an appointment with a psychiatrist.

The next morning, Natalie got up early. She thought about therapy and wondered if it would even help her. "Hey mom, could you drive me?" Natalie asked, rubbing her eyes.

"Yeah, of course," she said as she got up off the couch to change clothes.

Natalie looked outside, through her sliding back door, at the snow flurries. The snow was a surprise, there wasn't any in the forecast, so they had to move fast. Within an hour, the snow picked up and was accumulating on the sides of the road.

Natalie got in the car and laid her head up against the window. Staring at the trees as they drove by. Every few minutes, she glanced at the time on the dashboard, making sure that they weren't going to be late.

Natalie felt a little bit of relief that morning, knowing that she could finally get the help she was looking for. Her family was very supportive, but it was not enough to help her heal. She needed structure and a plan for her to heal properly. When they arrived, she had hope that it would help her understand all of her emotions and process some things she hadn't talked about.

Natalie and her mother got out of the car and went inside. Natalie sat down in the waiting room while her mother checked her in. She played with her thumbs and kept her head down, as she nervously waited to be called back. The clock was ticking and the crowd in the waiting room was starting to thin down. Finally, The large white office door opened, and a nurse stepped out. "Natalie" she said.

She stood up and became overwhelmed with fear. She considered backing out as they were checking her blood pressure. The nurse told her to get up and brought her into a room and down a long dark gray hallway. The psychiatrist's office was on the left.

"You're here to see Dr. Oliver, right?" The nurse asked before opening the door.

"Yes," Natalie replied.

The Nurse opened the door, and sat her down in a leather chair. She turned on a television, confusing Natalie and making her more nervous than before. "He lives in North Carolina and is here once a month. Other days, he does appointments through video chat," The nurse explained as she stepped outside. "If you have any questions don't be afraid to ask," she said, shutting the door.

Natalie sat there in the chair, trying to relax as best she could. She felt so awkward. She could see him, but he was typing before he spoke. There was an awkward silence while waiting for the doctor to speak to her. She sat there nervously, watching him type notes on his computer. "Am I supposed to say something?" Natalie thought, but ultimately decided to remain silent. The therapy office was not what at all what she expected. It was really small and there was only enough space for two chairs. The room was dimly lit and a little eerie. Natalie took off her jacket and put it in the dark red leather chair beside of her. After about a minute and thirty seconds of silence, he looked up at her and smiled.

"Are you Natalie?" Dr. Oliver asked, smiling.

"Yes, I'm Natalie," She answered, stuttering because she was caught off guard.

"Do you go by Natalie or something else?"He asked.

"I go by Natalie,"

"So, Natalie, What brings you here today?" Dr. Oliver asked, with a smile on his face.

Natalie paused for a moment and sighed, dreading to speak about what happened. She swallowed the lump in her throat "My fiancé was killed in a car accident about three weeks ago," she said as her voice cracked and she started to cry.

The psychiatrist looked back at her, smiled and gave her a minute to calm down. "I know it's still painful, but look at it this way. I bet it feels better today than it did three weeks ago,"

"Yeah, I guess it does,"Natalie said, sniffling.

"Right, things get better with time," He reassured her. "This might make you a little uncomfortable, but I have to ask for medical reasons. Are you having any suicidal thoughts?" He asked.

"Yes, yes I do. I don't feel like I have a reason to live anymore," Natalie answered, feeling like something was wrong with her.

"Are there any weapons in the house?"

"Yes, several, but I don't have access to them. There's no way I can get access to them. They're in a safe and I don't know the access code to open it," Natalie said.

Natalie changed the subject and started telling him about her vivid nightmares and flashbacks. He assured her that was normal and diagnosed her with PTSD. Her heart stopped, but there was no denying that she had severe trauma from Jason's car accident.

The thoughts of being behind the wheel again was scary, even riding in the car was difficult now. She had a hard time explaining that fear to people, because they didn't understand. When she did open up, people would always say they most unhelpful things like "You have to get on with your life at some point,"

"Is it normal to be so scared of driving like this?" She asked the curly haired psychiatrist.

"Yeah, it's extremely common. Most people have a fear like that after a tragedy like this occurs," Dr. Oliver said. Natalie's face lit up, feeling relief upon hearing his words. She wasn't crazy, she was damaged.

"Okay, so I'm gonna put you on Zoloft and some stuff for your anxiety attacks. I also want to see you back in two weeks. Before you go, promise me that you won't hurt yourself while you're gone?"

"I promise," Natalie said, smiling.

"Okay, Great. See you in two weeks,"

Natalie got her jacket and left in good spirits. She felt better, but knew there was a long way to go and a lot of work to do on her part to get better. Natalie sat down in the car, completely worn out. There's something about sharing her feelings that made her tired. She had a smile on her face, and her mother noticed, giving her lot of hope.

 Natalie came home and threw her jacket down on the kitchen table. She kicked her shoes off as soon as she walked through the door and practically ran into the living room. She fell back on her brown plushy couch and sank down slowly down in the comfort of the cushions. Natalie started up at the ceiling, turning the light on in the dim lit living room.

"Okay, so what's the next step from here?" She asked her mother, without skipping a beat.

"Have you considered going back to work? Translate some more books," her mother suggested.

"Yeah, but I'm afraid. Rereading those pages if going to be so hard," she explained.

 Natalie realized that she was going to have to finish the projects she started. She signed a contract and was not going to get out of it. She sighed and thought about what it would be like to take this next big step. She was so scared of it. "At least I'll have something to do during the day to keep me busy," she thought, trying to make herself feel better about it. She reclined back on the couch and groaned. about the change.

She did not have much energy, and concentrating was still really hard. She truly didn't think she was ready. Natalie's biggest fear was remembering the night Jason died. She spent time working instead of paying attention to him. She also was afraid to face her contractors and the authors she was working under. They would looking at her different and treat her different because of what happened. She had not spoken to her contractors since the night of the accident, telling them that Jason had died."Why does my life have to go on?" She questioned. "I don't want it to go on and no one understands or cares. I just want this life to be over, I want all of this to be over. Why did my life have to be like this?" Natalie thought, desiring to be able to express how she really felt and be understood.

Accepting grief now as a part of her everyday life, Natalie knew that getting back into a normal routine would be the best for her. A part of her was excited to be rebuilding her life, but she was scared of moving on. "What if I forget about Jason?" She thought, leaning with her head over her knees. Letting go of him was hard. Especially, since she couldn't go a day without thinking of him. Everything she did, he was on her mind.

Natalie took a deep breath and decided that she was going to start working again the next day. She got up and set her alarm clock for nine in the morning. "I need to get ready for bed," she thought, sighing. She felt heavy and went to wash her face. She finished up and sat down on the edge of her bed. "Oh Lord, I don't know if I can do this. Like you actually care about me though," she scoffed. Natalie fluffed her pillows and fell back forcefully onto the mattress and mentally prepared herself for the next day. She thought about her life and debated on whether or not this is what she was meant to do. Her future was uncertain, as she examined every single part of her life."I don't want to do this anymore," she thought, turning the lights off beside of her. She turned back over and stared up at the ceiling. "Is translating truly what I want to keep doing for the rest of my life?" She questioned herself, debating on what she would do if she did quit. She just wanted to be happy and seriously considered backing out of everything to sleep in. "Oh God, I have to get up and do this," She sighed, trying to motivate herself.

    Natalie laid in bed and for a while, unable to sleep. She tried shutting her eyes and relaxing, but the more she tried to force herself to sleep, the more restless she became. Frustrated, she got up and stretched, hoping to tire herself out. She wanted to forget about it so badly that she debated quitting all together. After pacing her bedroom floor for an hour, she looked at the clock and noticed that it was two in the morning. She took some medication to make her sleep, that was the only thing that was going to work and it did. Within thirty minutes, she was out.

"What's that noise?" She asked herself, still dreaming. No answer was given and no noise could be located. Finally she jolted awake. "Oh no, that's the alarm clock,"

She pulled the covers back and got up out of the bed, swallowing her pride and forcing herself to do this. Knowing that she was going to be down a while, she went to the kitchen to grab a bite to eat and set up a work space. No one else was up yet, except her cat that was trotting around the house like a show pony. The bright sun was peeking through the window blinds and the living room was in a peaceful silence. She went into the kitchen and got two slices of bread and put them in the toaster. She put her toast on a plate and brought it into the living room with her. Her laptop was sitting on the floor, next to a stack of magazines charging. She took a deep breath and picked up her computer and sat it in her lap. She took a deep breath and opened it "I can do this," she thought as she pressed the power button. The screen came on and her body began to shake, knowing that this was the first time she had seen these documents after Jason died.

She opened up a file titled, "How to be filled with the Holy Spirit" something she had spent a lot of time working on. She closed her eyes, afraid of the memories that she would encounter reading through the pages."I can't do this. I can't do this,I cannot do this!" She thought, as she turned her focus to something else for a moment.

She read through one paragraph and closed her computer. Tears were streaming down her face. "I can't translate something that I don't believe anymore," she thought as she got up and walked away to clear her mind. "I really don't think I can do this," she said as she looked down at her cat who was rubbing her feet. She thought for a moment about whether she should continue, but ultimately decided to take a break for a little while. "I am definitely not going to push myself," she thought as she went back to the couch and pulled herself together, gently leading herself back into it.

A couple hours later, She couldn't take it anymore and she quit for the day, she didn't know how much time she needed. She wanted the world to end and her situation to change.

In her soul, she felt like the only only person that could help her was Jesus, regardless of how mad at him she was. hen just shrugged it off as nerves and went to get ready for bed.

Natalie picked up her laptop from the floor next to her, reviewing the word documents that she had saved containing her manuscript translations. Reading through the pages brought back memories of Jason. The last time she had worked on the manuscript was the night before Jason died. She spent most of her time with Jason, which included her working time, and seeing that reminded her of him. "Do I really want to keep doing this?" She asked herself out loud.

Natalie fell asleep on the couch from extreme exhaustion. She woke up at one in the morning to a dead computer and a sore neck. She yawned and stretched, "oh my God." She said, getting up off of the couch and getting ready to go to bed. She sighed and laid down in the bed. Her back cracked in three separate places, feeling a small amount of euphoria before she began to feel left out. One of Jason's friends met a woman at the church both Natalie and Jason went to. He married her within a short amount of time and that bothered her so deeply. "I'm glad I had to give up everything I loved so others could be happy," Natalie said bitterly.

A pain shot through her chest that felt like her heart exploded. For the first time in her life, she truly felt like God had forsaken her.

"God, why did you take away what I wanted and give it to everyone else?" Natalie asked, she was angry, and what happened to her wasn't fair. She just wanted to be happy and there was nothing that could make her happy. She cried for a while, waiting on God to give her a response, but he didn't. "Lord, please don't be silent right now," she thought, God was completely silent fueling her to go from anger to absolute rage. She paused for a moment before speaking up again "You know, that wasn't fair God. After everything I've done for you, this is what you do to me! And you won't even give me a reason as to why you did it!"

Natalie sat back down into the couch that was behind her. In tears, she sat at looked at the floor questioning "Why me?" before finally collecting her thoughts and pulling herself together.

Chapter 7

Time passed and spring had sprung. The fields behind her house were a gorgeous shade of green. The scent of the fresh air warm air brushed up against Natalie's nose as she opened the kitchen windows. The change in the weather was a literal breath of fresh air. "It's such a beautiful day today," Natalie said.
"That it is," her sister responded from behind her.

The bright spring sun shone through the house, giving it a beautiful glow. They left the windows up, letting the fresh air into the house. An array of scents from blooming flowers filled the house. Natalie was excited, for the first time in a very long time. "It's too pretty of a day to sit inside the house," she thought, and decided to go outside. The sound of frogs croaking graced Natalie's ears. She loved that sound because it meant it was spring.

    Natalie went to the barn, and petted the animals. She was feeling good from the beautiful day and she was enjoying it. Her therapist encouraged her to get out in the sun more, because it would lift her mood. She took the advice and used the warm weather to her benefit. She enjoyed herself, seeing sights and the blooming trees. She finished feeding the goats, and came home exhausted, covered in dirt. She was happy, and her heart was filled with joy. The bright sunshine began to set over their farm, and everything felt different. It was like a different world.

    With the turn of spring, Easter was approaching. Natalie loved Easter. It was her favorite holiday and held such a special meaning to her. To her surprise, she was actually looking forward to it. The only downside were the large crowds of people that would be at church. She never liked large crowds, but since Jason died, she hated them a lot worse. People stared at her, no matter where she went, because they knew what happened to her. It was something that still bothered Natalie and no one understood.

Natalie was able to occupy herself, thinking about all the Easter festivities.
Sooner than she realized, Good Friday was upon her.

That morning she woke up and she was so excited. She jumped up out of bed and ran to her closet to pick out an outfit. She was getting ready to attend the annual Good Friday service. It was a rainy morning, but she was going to go to church anyway. She fixed her hair and put makeup on, genuinely feeling good as she grabbed her purse and came into the living room.

Natalie's mother was already in town, and she was going to meet her with her father and Kelcie. When she got to the church parking lot, the rain had slowed down a little. Natalie stepped outside of her father's pickup truck and struggled to open her umbrella. The water on the gravel in the parking lot made it slick and hard to walk. She finally made it to the door and was greeted by her pastor.

"Oh look, there's a celebrity among us today," he said jokingly, sticking out his hand to shake hers.

"That's exactly right," Natalie responded, playing along with his joke.

She went into the sanctuary and sat down in the back row of pews next to her father and her sister. To Natalie's surprise, there was a guest pastor, from Pike county, who would be preaching the sermon.

The service began with prayer and the whole congregation stood up. Natalie bowed her head and stared at the carpet on the floor thinking about taking a nap. When she sat back down and tried to focus. About halfway through the sermon, the children at the end of the pew were being loud and rowdy. "I can't here anything," Natalie thought, getting irritated and wanting to leave.

Suddenly, the preacher said "Our community mourns the loss of a beloved police officer, and I'm sure you all can relate to that. Didn't you all have a firefighter to get killed recently?" This got Natalie's attention and it felt like a dagger went through her heart.

Everyone inside the church looked at her, with that same sympathetic look that everyone gave her when they saw her. It made her so uncomfortable that she sank down in the pew. She prayed that the service would hurry and end.

"Out of everything in this sermon that I've not heard, that's the words I get to hear?" She thought, taking a deep breath to hold back her tears.

"Why would he bring something like that up?" She thought, rubbing her forehead in frustration.

She kept checking her phone, checking the time, because the clock was on the wall behind her and she didn't want to turn around. "Oh Lord, please don't let me suffer in this place much longer," she prayed.

For the rest of the service, She couldn't focus on anything else. After that everything the pastor spoke was just a blur. Finally, after what seemed like seven years, the closing prayer was said, and church was dismissed.

Out in the vestibule, people gathered around her and rubbed her back, telling her how sorry they were for her loss. She hated it, and left the church practically running.

On the way home, she became focused on her and Jason's upcoming wedding day."It's still two months away," Natalie told herself, trying to keep from crying. She was already upset that things were going the way they were, her day went sour fast.

On the way home, she became focused on her and Jason's upcoming wedding day. "It's still two months away," Natalie told herself, trying to keep from crying. She was already upset that things were going the way they were, her day went sour fast. God was distant to her and she still didn't want any type of a relationship with Jesus.

"It just doesn't make sense as to why someone else can get married, but I can't," she thought, urging her parents to hurry up and get home. She was anxious and she just wanted to lay down. She didn't like people patting her shoulder even before Jason died. "I wish my life was different," she thought. She barely spoke on the rest of the way home. She was so lost in thought that she couldn't speak. These thoughts brought up feelings of depression once again.

Natalie got home, kicked her shoes off at the back door and ran as fast as she could to her room. Her room was a mess, stressing her out even more. "I've really got to clean," she thought, falling back into her bed. She groaned when she hit the mattress, looking for motivation to do the massive amounts of laundry. "I have so much laundry to do," she cried, knowing good and well that she wasn't going to do it right then.

Grief covered Natalie like a heavy blanket. Her heart was hurting, thinking about what should have been. "At least he's gets to celebrate the resurrection with Jesus this year," she thought, trying to see the positives of it. She felt a little jealous that he was up there in heaven and she was still on Earth. "Why is it fair that Jesus gets to celebrate with him, but I can't?" She questioned, starting to cry.

Natalie rolled over on her back and started questioning a lot more. "Lord, why could you raise Lazarus from the dead, but not Jason?" she asked, thinking back on the day's sermon. It just didn't make sense. Everything she learned in church simply just didn't make sense, so she assumed it wasn't true. "I don't know what's true and what's not anymore?" Natalie thought, sitting up in bed tormented by thoughts and frustration.

Before she realized it, Easter Sunday came in what seemed like the blink of an eye. Natalie woke up extra early that Sunday. She was excited once again, hopeful that she wouldn't hear anything about Jason today. For once, she was going to focus on herself and try to have a good time. She got ready to go, putting on a white dress she bought specifically for the occasion.

As expected, the church parking lot was already full by the time she got there and she got there early. Natalie noticed a familiar vehicle in the parking lot, but dismissed it as. Though it looked like her ex boyfriend, Zeke's, truck she realized it probably wasn't him. As she got closer to the entrance, she contemplated not going in. "What if it is him?" She thought, not wanting to deal with him.

"I really don't want to have to deal with that psychopath today. He just will not take no for an answer," Natalie thought, as she walked through the doors.

Zeke was a man who treated Natalie poorly before she met Jason. He was very manipulative and it was either his way or no way. It was mental abuse and Natalie broke it off with him in 2014. Since the breakup, Zeke has tried several times to get Natalie back.

Her mother noticed the silver pickup truck as well. "Stay close to us, we'll protect you," her mother said, knowing that it was him.

Kelcie walked in front her, in a neon pink dress that was so bright it hurt her eyes looking at it. As soon as Natalie stepped inside the church, there he was. She hid behind her family, hoping he wouldn't see her. "Oh Lord," Natalie sighed and kept her head down as she walked into the sanctuary and sat down in whatever pew was available. She found one in the middle of the church and sat down at the end next to the center aisle. Zeke saw her when he came in with his family and stared at her.

Natalie tried to hide the best she could, but he still kept staring at her. Every 10 minutes or so, he'd turn around in his pew and stare holes into her. Her aunt, who was sitting behind her leaned up and said: "See that Natalie, that right there's an example of what you don't want," she said, laughing trying to cheer her up a little bit.

The service started and they had their time of fellowship. During that time, everyone came up to Natalie, telling her how pretty she was. She hated it and wanted to leave. She didn't feel as beautiful as she was and didn't like everyone crowding around her to get a hand shake or a hug. If anything, she thought she was ugly. Natalie never saw herself as a beautiful woman, even though men would stare at her for hours when they saw her. If anything, she took it as nuisance and hated hearing the words "You're so beautiful,". Finally, fellowship ended and the final hymn was played.

 The main service started as usual.
"I ask that you would stand in honor of the reading of God's Holy word," the pastor said as the congregation stood up and started reading from the gospel of Matthew.

 Through the reading, Natalie noticed Zeke staring at her again. She sighed and looked down at the open bible trying to not to focus on him. "I just want to go home," she thought, sitting back down in her seat as the preaching began. Natalie was able to relax a little and things were fine for the remainder of service.

 When the service was over, she grabbed her purse and wanted to leave quickly. She stepped out into the aisle and couldn't leave as fast as she wanted. "Why is this line moving so slow?" She thought, as she slowly made her way through the large crowd of people.

Stepping out into the vestibule was like a breath of fresh air. The air was cool from air conditioning and she could breathe. Zeke was standing to the side, staring holes into the side of Natalie's head. "Why do these things always happen to me?" Natalie questioned, stepping to the side to speak to the pastor.

The pastor pulled her father to the side, "Does Natalie have anything to do with Zeke?" He asked out of concern.

"No, she doesn't. She quit that a long time ago,"

"Good. She doesn't need that. That boy needs help," he said.

Finally, Natalie made it out the door and the fresh air wrapped her and her white dress. "I can breathe," she thought as she relaxed and breathed a sigh of relief. Her mind quickly went to focusing on food as that was her family tradition. She was having a good time and was surprisingly okay.

"You know, Jim at church told me how he was going to get Jason to be the youth minister here," her father said. "Why did you tell me that?" Natalie said, feeling her heart break into a million pieces.

It started to rain and Natalie was over it already. She felt left out and abandoned. Everyone was having a good time, but her. She didn't belong anywhere and no one understood. Her family wanted her to have a good time with them, but she just didn't feel like it. "I'm so ready to go home," she thought, praying that the day would end.

Just when it seemed like all hope was lost, the day finally came to an end and Natalie finally got to go home to rest.

Chapter 8

April had passed and the days seemed to never end. It had only been four months, but it felt like a life time. It was May, and Natalie's birthday was approaching, but she kept it in the back of her mind. She tried not to think about it, as she put some dirty laundry into a basket. The thoughts of celebrating her birthday without Jason were painful. She wanted to skip it and treat it like every other day, but she knew that wasn't going to be an option. Her family treated birthdays like holidays and not one was looked over, even if they didn't want to celebrate.

Though she used to love seeing her birthday come around, this year she despised everything about it. Her birthday only reminded her that God put her on this planet and she didn't want to celebrate something God did. All she did throughout her life was suffer and throwing a party for that was pointless.

The day that she dreaded since Jason died was coming too quickly. Though it was May, June sixteenth was uncomfortably close. "How am I going to get through this?" She thought, feeling the pressure of turning twenty three years old and still not being married, and having her almost wedding date coming up. Being single at her age was uncommon in the rural area where she lived. She felt like a failure. The time seemed to pass so slow, but too fast at the same time. Natalie wanted to hurry and get through this and the grieving process.

She managed to feel a little excitement about her birthday. It marked a new beginning and the start of a new journey. She thought about the memories of last year when Jason threw her a surprise party. It was the nicest thing anyone had ever done for her. For a week, he led her to believe that he wasn't going to be there for her birthday because of something with work. She was disappointed, but she understood the circumstances. She wasn't expecting a party at all, she wasn't even expecting him to be home and the surprise she felt seeing that made her love him even more.

Natalie's heart ached, thinking of those memories, wishing she could have that again. She felt so empty "I serious took that for granted. God, I miss him so much," she thought. Her demeanor changed from happy to depressed. "I'm never going to find anyone who will love me like that ever again," she thought, making herself come to terms with knowing she may never find anyone again. There were so many memories she had of him, but memories weren't enough. She felt alone, because no amount of support on Earth could help her.

It was the day before Natalie's birthday and her anxiety skyrocketed to an all time high. She kept her regular therapy appointment, so she could talk through it and describe what she was feeling. If she wasn't thinking about going through this year without Jason, she was thinking about her wedding date. She couldn't concentrate on anything else.

That evening when things were going smoothly, Natalie was called into the living room by her mother. "What do you want to do for your birthday this year?" She asked.

"I don't know, I'd rather just skip it altogether and not worry about it," Natalie answered, hoping thyme would let her skip it.

"Oh now, you can't do that. How about we have a small party? Just the family and a cake, no one else,"

"Why? What's the point? I don't enjoy my birthday anymore, it's nothing but a painful reminder that Jason isn't here with me anymore,"

"I know, but you can't give up and stop living," her mother said, attempting to be optimistic.

"I guess you're right," Natalie admitted and sighed.

    Natalie finally agreed to let them have a party. They weren't going to shut up until she agreed to it. Her family were known for their celebrations, so skipping her birthday was not an option. Frustrated, Natalie sat down in a bar stool at the kitchen island and just stared out the window.

    The next morning, Natalie woke up early and headed to the kitchen. She tried not to acknowledge that it was her birthday, and treated it like any other day. She didn't check her phone or the calendar. The tenth of May was just over looked that year, in her mind. In the kitchen, she helped her sister cook breakfast and enjoyed the time with her family. It was an absolutely beautiful spring morning, the birds were chirping and the sun was shining bright.

"Come here, I want to show you something," her mother said. Excited, Natalie made her over to the couch where she was sitting.

"What is it?" Natalie asked, cheerfully walking over to her mother who was pulling up her phone.

"This is Jason's tomb stone. The put it in today, and they wanted to get your opinion on it," her mother said, showing the phone to Natalie. Her heart shattered into a thousand tiny pieces.

"Why did you have to show me that today?" She asked, as flashbacks of the crash intruded her thoughts. She took the phone and looked at the images. It was a beautiful black polished stone with Jason's picture engraved in it and a white cross beside of it his picture. Looking at the images didn't seem real. Tears started to well up in Natalie's eyes. She handed the phone back to her mother and went back to the kitchen.

"Of all the days for this to happen, why did it have to be today?" Natalie asked, crying.

"I know," Her mother said.

The day was already starting off on the wrong foot, but she was still going to try and enjoy herself anyway. Natalie calmed down and got excited for rest of the day, thinking of things she could do to keep her occupied. As usual, her father ran to the mailbox as soon as it was delivered. He came in with the mail. "So what did we get in the mail today?" Natalie asked.

"Well, you got something, but you might not want to see it," her father said.

"Oh," she said as got up and got the stack of mail that he laid on the edge of the kitchen table. There was a card in the stack and it was addressed to her. She picked it up and opened it. It was from Jason's grandparents.

"What's going on in there? You got awfully quite all of a sudden," Her mother asked, joking around.

"Yeah…. I got a card from Jason's grandparents."

"Let me see," her mother said, as she came running into the kitchen excited.

Inside was a note written on the card and a fifty dollar bill. The note was sweet and thoughtful, telling her that it was okay to move on with her life when she was ready. Natalie teared up when she read the last part. "Thank you for making our grandchild's life wonderful," She loved those two old people more than anything in this world. They were such good people.

The idea of her birthday made her happy. She enjoyed spending time with her family and any excuse to eat cake was a good one, but it was just another painful reminder of how Jason was no longer here anymore. Her family showed up to the house, an hour late. She didn't want to leave her house and that's what she got. Natalie also didn't want anything special. She just wanted it to end and be done with. She sat down at the table where they were everyone was sitting and she smiled, putting on a brave face so no one could see the pain that was going on behind the scenes.

"Well, do you feel any older?" Her grandmother's new husband asked.

"To be quite honest with you, I don't feel a bit different," Natalie responded, laughing as she cut a piece of cake.

Natalie ate, trying to draw attention away from her. If she didn't eat, her parents would say something and she was tired of hearing that. She had heard all her life that she needed to eat more, but now it was worse. She was fine and she knew she was, but they didn't.

The party finally ended, at nine in the evening. She went and took a long shower, letting the hot water beat on her back. It cleared her thoughts mind and relaxed her. She finished showering and went back into the living room where her family was, looking for something to drink.

Natalie sat down on the couch and thoughts of what happened filled her mind. She thought it was odd that there had been no accident report to come up in four months since the accident. Natalie was aggravated, and she wanted answers. She talked with her parents about it, but deep down she knew Dustin wasn't innocent, but she desperately wanted to believe that he was.

Jason cared a lot for Dustin. He spent many nights praying for him, and even went to his high school graduation. He caused a lot of trouble in the fire department with other members, but Jason always came in as the peacemaker and defended him as he smoothed things over.

Natalie had this feeling in the pit of her stomach that something wasn't right. When something was off, she always knew it. It was the middle of May and Jason was killed in January. "Oh Lord, please don't let this county try to cover this up like they've done with everything else," she thought. It was only supposed to take a few weeks to get an accident report back, not months. Something was wrong and she was left with more questions than answers.

This tormented everyone who was affected by Jason's death. Deep down, everyone knew what happened, but there was nothing anyone could do about it yet. It was no secret that the county has covered up people's deaths before. It's well known throughout the entire state. However, Natalie tried to stay positive and told herself that was unlikely. Many people had told her that it could take up to six months to get an accident report, and that eased her mind. Natalie also believed that they weren't smart enough to cover up a death like this because it was so obvious what happened.

Later that week, her sister's high school prom was coming up. Natalie was chosen to do Kelcie's makeup and she was excited. She enjoyed makeup and had waited for this for a long time. Kelcie picked out a beautiful blue southern belle style dress that was trimmed with lace. Early that Saturday morning, Natalie got up and all of her makeup together and cleaned up her vanity, as she waited on Kelcie to get back from getting her hair done.

Kelcie made it home and came into her bedroom and she began doing her makeup.

"Do you want Gold or rose Gold eyeshadow?"

"I don't think rose gold would look right with my blue dress," Kelcie said.

"Girls, what are you all doing?" Her mother asked.

"I'm standing here putting Kelcie's makeup on," she responded.

"Your dad's cousin Ron is out here campaigning with him,"

Natalie instantly tensed up, clenching her teeth and gripping onto the makeup brush in her hand. Her heart almost stopped, and sped up to an unhealthy speed. She held so much hatred towards him, and she wanted nothing more to do with him. It angered her that her parents wouldn't tell them that none of them were welcome on this property anymore. Natalie took a few deep breaths and continued to apply her sister's makeup.

Her father came in the kitchen as Natalie finished up. Kelcie went to change. Her father was in the kitchen, standing with back up against the island. Natalie had several questions to ask. "What did he say?" Natalie asked.

"He was asking if we heard anything. He's been trying to figure out what's taking so long about the accident report. He even admitted that it was Dustin's fault,"
"Did you ask him why Dustin was still in the fire department?"
"No, I didn't. I completely forgot about it,"

Natalie was upset, but she didn't say anything. "Don't vote for him in the election," Natalie said. Making it clear that she was not supporting him. Natalie left the kitchen and went to go get ready herself. She was so broken and so betrayed by her own family.

Natalie came home that night, completely exhausted and depressed. Seeing all the young girls in their dresses reminded her of her wedding dress that she never got to wear. She began to cry, thinking about her upcoming wedding date. The thoughts of having a wedding date and not being able to get married scared Natalie. It just wasn't right. "All I wanted was a husband Lord," she said. "Why did you take him away from me?" She asked, worrying that she won't be able to make it through that dreadful day.

The 16th of June was vastly approaching and she hand to accept it. Natalie sighed and just went to sleep. Sleeping the rest of the day away. All she saw was the day of what almost was. Depressed, the next day, Natalie went to go see her therapist.

"What am I gonna do to get through this?" She asked. "My best advice is for you to try and go on a vacation," her therapist answered.

Natalie smiled, but realized that the idea of a vacation would be a stretch with her parents, but she took her therapist's orders anyway and thought of places to go. "I truly hope that we can go on a vacation," she thought. She never mentioned a word to her parents until she got home and put them both together in the same room. She gathered her parents and she suggested planning a vacation to them.

"So, my therapist recommended that I take a vacation to help me get through the wedding date," Natalie said, with her hands between her legs waiting for a response.

Her father was not amused, but her sister and mother were okay with the idea.

"I really want to go to the beach," Natalie suggested.

"I hate the beach. You get sand in everything," Kelcie chimed in, sharing her opinion.

"But I love the beach,"

"Why? It's awful. The water is salty, the sand gets everywhere and no matter how much sunscreen you use, you still get sunburned," Kelcie said.

"You're just still upset over that time you swallowed ocean water at myrtle beach," Natalie said, laughing, trying her best to persuade Kelcie to go to the ocean.

Ultimately, they decided to go mining for gemstones in North Carolina. Natalie wanted to go to the Virginia safari park, but that was a hard no from the rest of her family.

The most anticipated day of the year in Magoffin County had finally arrived. Election Day. People lined up early, on that rainy Tuesday morning, at polls all across the county to cast their vote. It was an important election this year, since it was the time to elected county officials. Natalie despised this day. She hated county politics, because things were never done right and the only people who were elected were the same people who had been in office for thirty years. However, that day Natalie chose to do her part for the country, as her great grandfather always said "Never skip an election, it's your right as an American citizen,"

Natalie debated on whether she made the right choice or not. "Is it even worth going to vote?, they're going to cheat anyway." Natalie .

"Yeah, we need to go vote, we need to at least try to get the sheriff out of office." Her father said, unfortunately leaving Natalie without much of a choice. She got up and got ready, dragging her feet because she did not want to go.That Election Day was also the day of Kelcie's birthday. Her parents had planned a party for later that day and they were given the task of picking up things for the party, so Natalie and her family chose to go vote at noon.

By the time they got there, The parking lot was already crowded, with people standing outside the building campaigning with one another, which was not uncommon. It was a county race, so it was the only one that mattered to people in this county. Natalie sat in the truck and looked at the crowd. She sighed, losing all faith in humanity with just one glance. "Why do people love this corruption so much?" She thought to herself. Natalie got out of the truck, her sister following behind her, as they walked through the cold air to the entrance of the school.

Frustrated from the large crowds, she hid behind her sister, but she was unable to hide from everyone. Just when she thought she had success, someone she knew spotted her.

"Well hello there Mr. Jenkins," the man said to Natalie's father.

His wife came up to Natalie and hugged her while her father was still talking. "Lord, please help me. I just wanna go home," she thought.

When the woman left, Natalie had the lingering smells of her perfume on her shirt. She thought the day would never end. Finally, she made it to the registering table, when saw members of her family who were over the fire department where Jason volunteered in his spare time. Natalie's heart pounded, and her eyes went red with rage. She stepped back and took a deep breath, preparing herself for any conversation they may start. They stood and stared at Natalie. Not speaking a single word. What was once a close family relationship, was nothing anymore. Natalie's father tried to speak to them, but they did not make an effort to speak back to him. They rubbed up against him without even saying a word. Natalie was already mad at them to begin with, since they did not take Dustin out of the fire department after he killed Jason. Seeing them hurt her, but it hurt her even worse that they didn't speak. "They could have at least apologized." She thought. She didn't want to see them, but she knew she couldn't escape.

    Natalie left the school, fuming. Her face was blood red and hot to the touch. Her heart was pounding skipping beats and she walked sat down in backseat of her car. She didn't say a word until her body stopped shaking. "I can't believe I trusted them," she thought with her head leaning against the backseat. She took a deep breath and Natalie spoke up.

"I wonder why they wouldn't even speak to me," Natalie asked.

"Probably because when they see you, they're reminded of what they did," her mother responded.

"I can't believe he didn't even speak to me, and he rubbed up against me," her Father chimed in.

Natalie was hurt. She was betrayed by her own family. "They deserve to be scared when they look at me, after everything they've done," she thought, laughing with her sister who was equally as angry. "That's my family. I thought I could trust them." She said

"They've always been that way." Natalie's Father said

"Why though, weren't they close with grandpa?" Natalie asked.

"Not really. They usually only came to him when they needed something."

"Ah, he's just mad that you misspoke his name," Kelcie spoke up, laughing.

Natalie laughed through her pain, hiding it well with her sense of humor. At that moment, that's the only way she knew how to deal with it. Screaming wasn't going to help, neither was talking through it. The damage had already been done.

Natalie came home and was totally exhausted. from the election exhausted. There was a couple of hours until she had to be in town again, so she relaxed in the bed, almost falling asleep. Her mind started to wander the more she relaxed and it ultimately went back to feeling betrayed by her family. She was furious. "If they truly have nothing to hide, why are they acting this way?" She thought. Natalie wanted answers and she toyed around with the idea of changing her last name just so she would not have to be associated with them.

A thunderstorm was in the distance, and the rumbling thunder soothed her troubled mind. She took a deep breath and claimed herself down. Just as she was starting to doze off, Natalie was awakened by her mother busting through her bedroom door.

"Get up! It's time to go!" She exclaimed, waking Natalie up.

"Fine," Natalie grumbled as she got up and got dressed to head to town.

Chapter 9

The seasons had changed and fall had arrived. Fall was Natalie's favorite time of the year. It wasn't too hot or too cold. The sun was getting dim and the leaves were turning orange. It was late September, the twenty eighth day of the month to be exact. It was still hot outside, and didn't really feel like fall at all. Natalie was spending the day with some of her family that she had not seen in well over a year. Her aunts from Georgia. The family reunion was originally scheduled in April, a few months before the wedding, in order to break things up a little and give her parents a break from planning a wedding, a high school prom and moving to a new house. Since Jason died, they had to postpone it. Natalie also felt bad for holding things up. Her family were understanding and supportive, but it still made everything a little different because of her.

The first night, was the fun night. Going out to eat was always an enjoyable moment for Natalie, but she was a little hesitant to go out at first. "Is this really worth it?" She questioned, as she finished getting ready to go. As soon as she finished getting ready, the phone rang and it was her family wondering where they were. She had no choice but to go, so she decided to just forget about everything and enjoy her evening.

Natalie was surprised by the amount of people that came to the restaurant. People she hadn't seen in a long time. The restaurant was crowded, filled to the brim with people. "I am not staying here longer than I have to," Natalie told her parents as her anxiety began to rise. They looked at her and assured her that they wouldn't be there longer than she felt comfortable with. Large crowds made Natalie nervous and she was not about to push herself. She sat down, and smiled, putting on a brave face. Natalie's aunts got up and came over to hug her.

"How are you doing?" One of them asked.

"I'm doing okay. About as good as I can do," Natalie answered.

    She was not expecting this many of her family to show up. Most of them didn't show up until the second day, at their home. Natalie was in misery. The loud music, the people looking at her and the tight crowded space made for a miserable night.

    A few painstaking hours later and Natalie finally got to leave. She sat down the back seat of the car and gave the biggest sigh of relief.

"Was it that bad?" Kelcie looked over and asked.

"Yes! Yes it was that bad," Natalie responded. Their father came to the car and started the vehicle, their mother followed soon after them.

Natalie came home and immediately got ready for bed. The next morning seemed to come in a flash. The noise coming from the kitchen woke her up. She sat up, confused as to how the sun came up so fast. "I slept hard last night," she thought, slowly getting up out of the bed to fix her hair and makeup to prepare herself for the long day ahead. She came into the living room when she was dressed and she was surprised to already see people there. Around eleven that morning, people starting packing into her small home. She practiced the techniques that her therapist taught her. Trying to keep her anxiety to a minimum, and it worked.

However, around twelve the house was completely full. Natalie escapes to the den to deal with her social anxiety. Hiding was the only thing she knew to do at that point. She was able to relax, talking to her immediate family and solitude away from the hustle and bustle of everything else. After a few deep breaths, she regained her composure and a smile came across her face. For the rest of the day, she hid in the den, with her parents and her sister. The less she was around people, the better. One woman found Natalie and came up to her, asking what grade she was in. Natalie looked back at her confused "I'm not in school anymore. I haven't been for a while," she responded.

Natalie laughed, but deep inside she was upset. She hated being as old as she was and being mistaken for a sixteen year old. It happened most of her life, but it still made her feel ugly. The rest of the day, she day with a headache and a crushed spirit. "I just want this to end already. Maybe I wasn't ready for this," she thought. "It's time to eat!" She head someone scream.

Everyone in the house ran towards the kitchen table. Natalie took her time and waited for the line to thin down. She sat there, alone on her grandmother's couch in the den, rethinking her life's decisions. She missed

Jason. He attended with her last year and he for in well with her family. "My life has taken a complete a one hundred and eighty degree turn in just a matter of months," she thought. Though she missed him, she was thankful that she was no longer where she used to be at and she was starting to get used to being alone.

Natalie got up off the couch and walked into the dining room with her father behind her. People were talking amongst each other and the yard was full of people. Her home was so full of people who were chatting and having a great time, but Natalie was silently screaming. She hated it, she was bored and stressed. She also was worried that people would ask her questions about what happened to her. Some of her relatives were gathered in a circle looking at pictures of her father as a child.

"Oh My God, Natalie, you have to come look at this!" Kelcie screamed across the room.

Natalie went walked over to her and looked down at the Polaroid photo. It was her father laying on a German Shepard dog.

"Daddy, I don't ever want to hear you say how much you don't care about dogs again," Natalie told him

"This must be where you get it from," Kelcie added, who hated animals.

Natalie and Kelcie went back to the den and she was relaxed again, enjoying herself and cracking a few jokes. Suddenly, her happiness was interrupted when something caught her eye. She looked up and was shocked to see who was there. "Oh no," she said, in a panicked tone.

"What is it?" Kelcie asked.

"You know who is here,"

"Of course, you dreamed it. Your dreams always come to pass," she said.

It was a distant cousin of hers, that had a connection to the fire department. He walked by the door and came in the house. She was furious.

"I thought I told you that not to invite any of them!" Natalie addressed her father.

"I didn't actually think they would show up," her father responded. Natalie took a deep breath, she didn't want to be angry at her father, even though she begged him to tell his family not to invite them. Natalie's heart sank to her stomach and she shook her head. "Here we go," she said, angry.

Her heart was pounding when they came inside. Her grandmother got up and immediately ran over to them. She shook their hands, and led them into the kitchen, trying to keep the situation under control while Natalie watched silently from the den. The more she watched, the angrier she got. Her heart was pounding so hard she could hear it.

"I'm going talk to them!" Natalie said.

"Natalie, don't. You won't be helping anything," Kelcie said, pulling her arms to keep her from going into the kitchen. She walked Natalie over to chair, trying to help her calm down. "I'll let you go talk to them when you're calm, but for now, Mamaw can talk to them,"

Natalie took a deep breath, trying to calm herself down. "I can't get too worked up," she thought. Natalie's grandmother brought up the question that had been burning on her mind for months.

"So, do you know if Dustin is out of the fire department?" The grandmother asked.

"As far as I know, he's still in it. I really don't know though." He responded.

The conversation continued and eventually came back to Dustin once more.

"Oh, they got black box back, it said that Dustin had a truck malfunction." He said.

"That's actually not true." Natalie's Grandmother spoke up. "There's actually never been an accident report to come back." She added.

Her cousin, looking confused, did not believe her at first.

"What? He just says he's so hurt over what he did,"

Natalie heard what was said and she was taken aback. Natalie paused for a moment, trying to process the words she had just heard, then spoke up in anger. "Okay… first things first, he didn't just hit his best friend, he killed his best friend. Secondly, there has never been anything to come back about what happened to Jason Tackett. Dustin is as guilty as guilty as sin."

The family were cleaning up after most of the people left. A close family friend to them pulled Natalie over to the side.

"I hope you find a good man that will treat you as good as the last one," she said, patting her on the back.

"Yeah…" Natalie responded, trying not to be rude.

Natalie was infuriated and couldn't wait for the rest of them to go home. She escaped to her room, her safe place. She closed the door and leaned up against the bright pink walls, taking a deep breath, she slid to the floor in the exhaustion. "Well, John Brown's dead and the big day's over," she heard her father say from the other room. She couldn't stop herself from laughing. Every year, he says that stupid phrase. It helped her relax.

She finally got up off the floor, changed her clothes, took her dry crusty makeup off her face. She flopped down on her bed and just rested. Her body physically hurt from being on her feet all day, and her body laying against her fresh clean sheets felt like heaven.

Natalie laid, resting and remembered the pain she endured over the months. Her heart was broken, but seeing them made her feel different. She truly believed that they didn't have anything to do with it, considering that it was his brother who was in charge of the fire department. She couldn't help but think about how her own family would support a criminal over her. "How could they do this to me? I trusted them," she thought on the brink of tears.

Natalie sat up, unable to sleep. She got her little brown leather covered journal and wrote her feelings. Halfway through, she stopped and stood up, looking out the window and the beautiful night sky. The moon was full and the stars filled the sky. She could feel a change in the atmosphere. She laid her head up against the wall and smiled. Her life was no longer dull and she felt like she had a purpose again. She was genuinely happy.

What started out as writing to relieve stress and feelings, eventually turned into a full fledged book over the course of two months. Late one fall night while Natalie was writing she had a cray idea. "I think I'm going to turn this into a book and publish it," she thought. At first, she thought the idea was crazy, that no one would be interested in her story. She battled these feelings back and forth for a while, before finally deciding to start looking for a publisher.

Natalie was just about to start a brand new career. One that she had always dreamed of. Natalie finished her manuscript, and found a publisher she liked after weeks of searching the internet. She debated on submitting the manuscript, but ultimately decided to do it. She felt like God wanted her to do it. Natalie waited weeks to hear back from the publisher about her manuscript. To the point that she forgot about it. It all started on one early Tuesday morning. Natalie was in bed, sleeping peacefully, all of a sudden, Natalie was awakened by a phone call. She reached over and picked it up, looking at the caller ID.

"Hello." Natalie said.

"Yes, May I speak with Natalie please."

"This is Natalie."

"Hi Natalie, this is Holly from the publishers and I'd like to tell you that we have decided to go through with the publishing."

"Oh my God, thank you so much." Natalie said, sighing with both relief and joy.

Natalie jumped out of bed and ran to Kelcie's bedroom. "Get up, we're going to Pennsylvania!" Natalie screamed.

"Huh?" Kelcie rose up and murmured. Natalie closed her bedroom door and ran into the kitchen and stood there, taking it all in. This was the happiest she had been in eight whole months. it was booming. Natalie so many exciting things coming up and other good things planned for the rest of the year. The one thing she was looking the most forward the launch of her first book. Natalie had planned the party in her spare time, she was so excited. Thinking of all the things she could do, she turned to the internet for inspiration.

Her new career took her to levels that she could have never imagined. Though things were changing, Natalie was beginning to grow tired of being pent up in the house all the time. She wanted to explore the world more, but mostly, she just wanted to meet someone else. Natalie took a deep breath and left her office space, heading to the living room where her family was.

Chapter 10

After a long a difficult couple of months, things had finally settled down and life was finally back to normal. Natalie was exhausted, but she finally woke up feeling completely rested on morning. She was full of energy and actually happy for once. She finally got caught back up on her sleep and worked out a good sleeping schedule that worked for her. Natalie got up and stretched, making her way into the kitchen with a new attitude this bright and cold Tuesday morning.

Natalie made her way to the box of cereal sitting on the kitchen counter. Pouring the cereal into the bowl was quickly interrupted when her cat became interested and stuck his head in the bowl.

"What are you doing buddy boy?" She asked, picking him up and moving him out of the way, trying to be quiet because her father was on the phone.

"Who was that?" Natalie asked when he hung up the phone.

"The telephone company, were moving today!" Natalie's Dad screamed at her as she walked over to the table.

"Huh?" Natalie said, confused because she thought the moving day would be a lot farther down the road.

"The telephone company is coming to hook up the internet today, so we have to move or we don't have internet and television,"

"Wait, why? Why today?" She asked, as her heart sank to her stomach.

"I didn't think they would do it this fast," he explained.

Natalie had been praying for a fresh start for a long time, but this came as a complete shock to her. She knew they were planning on moving. They had remodeled the house for a while. She knew the day was coming, but deep down she didn't really want it to. The change was scary and comfortable, but now she was left without a choice. Natalie was silent for a few hours, not knowing what to say or do. "Lord, when I asked you for a change, I didn't know you were planning this. I didn't want to move and you knew that," she thought. She took her fate, and decided that if this was God's will, then she was going to do it.

Natalie's mind quickly shifted from calm to panic, even though she knew they were planning this for a while. Natalie was completely against moving. She hated the idea of leaving her childhood home and no matter how much she begged, that wasn't an option. Natalie finished eating what she could and left the table. Upset, she leaned up against the wall and broke down into tears. "I don't want to do this," she thought as she began to panic. She took a few deep breaths and tried to process this brand new change. Her life was changing and it was changing fast. Nothing was the same anymore and it made her uncomfortable. Realizing that she didn't have a lot day, she got up and pulled herself together. She changed out of her pajamas, and started putting things into boxes.

    Natalie walked over to her closet and got a few scarves out. It was cold out, and she needed them for today and the next few days. She looked at them on the bed and got depressed, realizing what was happening. She put some shoes into a box and carried them out to the hallway, almost falling over a stack of books in her room. "Ouch," she said as she sat down on the floor, frustrated.

"Why did they choose today to do this?" Natalie asked, angry as her father walked to the back of the house.

"They didn't, I did. I just didn't think this would happen today," he responded.

"You won't die, maybe this will be good for you," Kelcie chimed in.

"I guess not. I'll have to suck it up and go on. I don't really have much else of a choice. You're also right, maybe this will be good for me," Natalie said, trying to make herself feel better.

Natalie sighed, and got up off the floor, this time moving the books out of the way. While cleaning, Natalie found some items that reminded her of Jason. She put them into a plastic container, and slid it away, trying to forget about it. "Today is that day," she thought. Natalie left the room, with tears in her eyes, to gather her thoughts once again. "This is going to kill me," she thought. She did not want to move and begged her parents for years not to make her move, but now she had no choice. Jason was gone and she had nowhere else to go.

It was very late November and winter had already made it its arrival. It was colder than usual and December was only four days away. Natalie opened up the front door and walked outside onto the cold concrete to take a break. She took a deep breath and stared at the brick house that wasn't too far in the distance. "I hate this," she thought, filling with anger that she was having to move. It was already decorated for Christmas, due to the thanksgiving celebration that had been held there just the week before.

Natalie started to cry. She was already under the stress of Christmas approaching. A holiday she once loved, now she hated. Now, with the impending fact that she was moving to a place that she hated definitely did not help in this transition. She went back inside and sat down on her bed, staring at the mess that had been made by going through all of her stuff. Natalie made the decision to try and remain as positive as she could be. "After all, I did pray for a new beginning," she thought, as she shook her head. "I just didn't want this to be the new beginning," she thought as she got up off her bed and started working again.

"What's so bad about moving anyway?" Kelcie asked.
"I just really feel like I'm not supposed to be there," Natalie responded.

Kelcie's question made her think for a minute. There was no logical reason as to why she felt the way she did about moving. "Why don't I want to move?" She asked herself genuinely not understanding why she felt they way that she did. For a few minutes, she couldn't think about anything else other than she felt like she wasn't supposed to be there. That home was supposed to be her grandmother's home and making it her own was a difficult transition.

"This year has literally been the worst year of my life," she thought. "I'm so done with everything changing," she thought as anger over took her. She began throwing items of clothing into boxes.

"This will be good for you. You'll be able to focus on other things for once and maybe get your mind off of everything that happened this year," her father said, trying to encourage her.

The thought of moving was still really painful. The only thing she asked for was just to stay where she was at. Her life was changing way too fast, and not in the way she wanted it to. Natalie started thinking of the positives and tried to be excited about starting a new life. Even though she did not want to, Natalie had no choice but to do so, in hopes that she could finally close this painful chapter of her life once and for all.

"I hope mice haven't been in these," she thought as she stacked up the boxes and struggled to carry them up the porch steps into the house. She knocked on the door with her foot, "Let me in," she screamed from the back door. Her father came over to her and let her in, throwing the boxes on the kitchen floor.

"I guess I'll need something to sleep in tonight," she realized. Natalie went over to her dresser and grabbed a few personal items that she was going to bring with her for the first night. She laid them out on her bed separately, along with her pajamas, underwear and regular clothes for the next day. "It's almost like a vacation," she thought, as she sighed. Realizing that trying to make herself happy wasn't working

She sat down on the floor in front of the closet door, going through everything that was in there. Storage containers of her toys from childhood, shoes and other random things that she had forgotten about. She got to the back of the closet and found a clear plastic storage container that was filled with things from her engagement and just Jason in general. She hesitated before opening it, but eventually she got the courage to look inside.

Natalie picked up an old photo album that contained pictures of the two of them that was given to her at his funeral. She put them away because the memories were too painful. There was also a picture frame that contained a picture of her in her wedding dress and she felt a knife being driven into her heart. She put the picture back inside the box and found the book that Jason had made for her as a Valentine's Day gift last year. She shut the lid on the box and got up out of the floor to examine it.

She smiled while she looked at it. It had been hidden underneath her red engagement dress and the banner that was on the side of the fire truck when he proposed, locked away in a storage container where it belonged.

She thought about it for a while as she put the rest of the things back inside and shoved the storage container to the back of the closet. "I'll deal with this another day. I can't handle this anymore," she thought as she felt her chest tightening from a combination of anxiety and grief.

Natalie held onto the book she pulled out of the storage container. She laid it down on the nightstand next to her bed, leaving it alone so she could finish doing other things. She sat down on her bed and stared at the book for a while. She did not know what to do with it. "Do I put it back up?" She questioned. She stared at the cover, thinking of all the good memories that it brought back. Tears welled up in her eyes as she thought about Jason. She missed him so bad that it physically hurt. She sat there for about five minutes before deciding not to put the book back up. She stopped doing the other things she was doing and focused on those memories. She paused for a moment, looking down at the book titled "Reasons Why" that she held in her hands.

"Should I look through it?" She thought. Natalie opened the book and started flipping through the pages, looking through the illustrations. They were stick figures of her and Jason together and above each one, were written the things that Jason loved about Natalie and their relationship.

She slowly closed the book, unable to bear reading the rest of it. Her chest hurt even though she didn't read too much of it. She opened it again, and started reading, little by little, unconsciously aware of it. Each of the pages were filled with the reasons why Jason fell in love with her. At the bottom of each page were cute stick figure drawings of Natalie and Jason. She sat there, flipping through the pages, looking at the drawing of her and Jason. Tears came to her eyes knowing that she was loved that much, and that great love was gone.

All of a sudden, Natalie was startled by hearing a knock at the door. "Oh no!" Natalie thought, "I can't let them see me upset," she quickly tried to pull herself together and stopped her crying on a dime.

"Who is it?" she asked, trying to hide her cracking voice. She turned around on the bed to look at the door, praying to God that they wouldn't know she was crying.

"Are you ready to go?" Kelcie asked as she stuck her head inside of the bedroom door from the hallway.

"Yeah, just give me a second!" Natalie said, quickly turning around and putting the book away as her sister came into her room.

"Come on, you're wasting the hours of daylight!" She said in a smart Alec tone.

Before her sister could get away from the door, Natalie said " Wait! I need you to help me carry these boxes to the truck, before it starts snowing.

Kelcie looked at Natalie and rolled her eyes, sighing "Fine! Give them here," she said, walking into Natalie's bedroom.

Kelcie picked up the stack of boxes that were next to the bed. There were only two boxes, but they were heavy with items. Natalie picked up the clothes off the foot of her bed and carried them along with Kelcie.

"Is that all you're going to carry?"

"Yes," Natalie laughed.

Kelcie rolled her eyes once again at Natalie. She decided to help anyway, thinking that it would take forever if she didn't. Natalie pushed most of the boxes, because they were too heavy to carry. It took a while, moving most of the boxes from the bedrooms to the kitchen. Natalie stood and looked at the kitchen that was full of boxes. "Life is so different now." She thought. Both sisters left out the front door with only a matress, a few toiletries, and some clothes. That night was the first night they would spend in their new home.

    They picked up a few small furniture pieces, ones that could be carried out easily, and put in the truck bed. Natalie put her clothes and things in the backseat next to her. Natalie say down in the tightly packed truck, wishing that she did not have to go. The pickup truck was completely loaded to the point that it was nearly impossible to fit anything else into the vehicle, even though it was just the bare necessities. Both sisters and their father piled into the truck.

"Thank God that this drive isn't too far from here, because if we try to fit anything else in here, it ain't gonna make it."Kelcie said from the passengers seat.

    Natalie laughed and shook her head, knowing how Kelcie's sense of humor was. Natalie was forced to sit in the backseat that was completely stuffed to the ceiling with boxes. There were barely two inches of seat left, which squished Natalie up against the door. Natalie's ride to their new home was an uncomfortable one, but thankfully, a short one. The gray Chevrolet pickup truck pulled into the yard against the front porch. Snow began to fall as soon as the truck engine shut off. Natalie and her father got out of the truck and made a way through, and by the time they were parked and situated, the yard was already covered with a thick heavy snow. Temperatures were dropping by the hour so they had to work extremely fast. Kelcie was grumbling to herself about having to unload things in the cold and snow, as Natalie stumbled out of the back seat, trying to keep the items from falling out onto the ground.

"Let's get the big stuff in first, we'll worry about the small stuff later." Natalie suggested after closing the truck door. Kelcie agreed, and started taking the large items out the truck bed.

"Natalie, I think we should get the television in first." Kelcie said

"You're probably right," Natalie agreed.

They went to the bed of the truck and moved items around so the television could be removed easier. Natalie grabbed one of the television and Kelcie looked at her confused.

"You're gonna try to lift the tv with your stick arms?" She asked, making fun of a Natalie's small stature because it was, not only, the heaviest thing to carry in, but it was also electronic, which couldn't get wet with the snow. The load started to get less and less until they were down to just personal clothing items, which were basically just for the night. When everything was moved into the house, the two of them fell down on the only couch in the entire house. They were worn out and extremely cold form the freezing temperatures outside.

"I'm killed!" Kelcie said, while reclining back on the couch, propping her feet up on the ottoman. Natalie tried to make herself more comfortable by changing into pajamas. The house was pretty much empty except for a few pieces of furniture and a bag of cat toys that Kelcie brought to help him adjust to the new house.

Natalie tried keeping herself occupied by interacting with her cat, but she could not keep her mind from wandering. An hour passed, and her mother came home from work, bringing food home with her.

Natalie became depressed, life was not the same anymore and Natalie wanted things to go back to the way they were. Memories of how good life used to be flooded her mind, "I really had it all, didn't I," she thought as she stepped away from the stove. Natalie's mother looked at her, wondering why she left.

"What are you doing?" She asked.

"Oh Nothing, I just stepped back for a minute," Natalie replied.

after the move, Natalie made herself comfortable in her room, and occupied herself by watching countless YouTube videos until she got sleepy. She stayed there for about thirty minutes, until sleepiness started to come upon each one of them. Natalie came back to watch the news and brush her teeth. All of them were nervous about sleeping in a place that had not yet become a home, especially Natalie's father. His way of dealing with the stress was petting their cat, over and over again.

Natalie finished brushing her teeth and looked at herself in the mirror. She had mixed emotions "Is this really where I'm supposed to be?" She thought. She left the bathroom and to put sheets on her mattress that was laying on the floor. She unfolded the sheets and struggled putting them on. After a few minutes she was out of breath and fell down on the bed to rest. She took a few deep breaths, and forced herself to get up and finish making the bed. Natalie's cat made his way into her room, and laid down on the floor. She closed the door, keeping her cat in the room and turn the lights off and the television on. The Nanny was on. Her focus was not on the 90's sitcom, but on her new life. "Lord, my old life is officially gone." She said out loud, scared of the future.

Natalie became overwhelmed with sadness that the life she had once known so well had gone away completely. "I just want things to go back to the way they were, Lord. It was easier back then," she cried, feeling like she had nothing. There was no comfort, only pain. The comfort that she once knew was gone, and she was all on her own. Even though the pain was intense, there was hope. She knew that things would get better and she was optimistic that maybe the hurt and grief could finally subside.

Eventually, Natalie fell asleep after hours of thinking. and woke up to the bright winter morning sunshine peeking through the blinds of her bedroom window. Natalie felt so strange, and she did not like it. Everything was different and a new life had begun in just twenty four hours. It didn't necessarily feel like a good change, but it was. Her new home was going to take some adjusting to, but nonetheless, somewhere deep inside of her, hope was finally coming back to her. after many long months of hopelessness. There was still one hurdle she had to get through, though, and that was Christmas. Christmas was approaching and it was her first one without Jason. It also served as a permanent reminder of how Jason proposed to Natalie, since it was on Christmas Eve. She hoped that being in the new house would her forget about that, and even considered skipping Christmas all together, but the memories were unfortunately, still there.

Chapter 11

Natalie was snoring soundly in her bed, resting comfortable in her new home. She was adjusting to it better than she thought, though she still wasn't happy with being here. Suddenly, the horrid sound of the alarm clock rang throughout Natalie's small pink bedroom. She jolted awake and groaned. She stretched her arm out to turn the clock off. "What time is it?" She asked, raising her head up, squinting her eyes. The clock said nine O'clock. She groaned once more, falling face first down in her pillow. "It's too early," she thought. She rose up and stretched. Her joints cracked, loudly and she enjoyed the euphoria. She got her phone and checked her email, before she realized what day it was.

She smiled with relief. It was a day she had looked forward to for so long, New Year's Eve.

"Thank God this year is over!" She said with a sigh of relief. The worst year of her life was finally over and Natalie couldn't describe how excited she was. She through the covers back and jumped up out of the bed. She was more than excited for the turn of the new year, knowing that the new year was going to be better.

Natalie skipped into the living room, with a huge smile on her face. Her heart was filled with joy and hope for the upcoming year, but most of all, she was overcome by relief that the worst year of her life was finally over. She sat down in the recliner, pulling out her phone to check her email. To her surprise, it was from her literary agent, informing her that the first round of editing was done on her book. Natalie was glowing and full of hope. Now she could close this chapter of her life, and hopefully start fresh.

2019 actually looked promising, she had a lot of new and exciting things heading her way, keeping her focused and motivated.

"Why are you so happy for?" Her father asked, looking at Natalie's enormous grin on her face.

"The first round of editing on my book was finished today," Natalie responded.

"How many mistakes did you make?"

"Quite a few actually," Natalie responded, jokingly knowing that he was making fun of her for how particular she is with grammar and punctuation.

Natalie looked down at her phone and scanned through her manuscript. Her days were now filled with things to keep her busy, so her mind wasn't wandering as much as it used to be. Something had changed in Natalie, that signified healing. She started feeling lonely and was considering the idea of dating again.

"I can't do that, I'm not ready," she thought, trying to get that thought out of his head. Natalie paused for a moment, and came to the realization that she was, in fact, single. She shook her head, trying to process the revelation. Her heart was pounding and her body was shaking. "That's the first time I've thought about that and not broke down," she thought.

The first step to fixing a problem is acknowledging that there is one, so she accepted it. The idea of dating came back into the picture, again and she was okay with it. Natalie was not meant to be single for the rest of her life and she knew that, but the idea of dating again scared her to death. The idea of being with someone new was nice, but she did not know where to start. She also didn't want her heart broken again. "I really shouldn't even have to be dating again," she thought, clenching her fists. She shook her head and tried to stop thinking about it and focused on her work.

She wanted to move forward, but she didn't want to focus on that just yet. Natalie smiled and enjoyed her rapidly changing life. There was still a fear of death that Natalie had suppressed deep inside of her soul. That didn't change the fact that loneliness was still there. She worked on her book for a little while longer, before finally getting mentally exhausted.

Telling people what happened to her made Her feel good. Writing about Jason's death was a great way to get her bottled up emotions out. The people who hurt her deserved to know how she felt, regardless of whether they cared about it or not. She was helping others by sharing her story, no matter who it rubbed the wrong way. Natalie began to worry after reading through the manuscript, it was only a week until the one year anniversary of Jason's death. She pushed that out of her mind.

Natalie spent most of the day, preparing for the party that evening. She was determined to have a good time and not think about the upcoming week. She stood in her room, putting some folded clothes away before she was got ready to go. She struggled folding a pair of jeans when her phone buzzed in her pocket. Her heart stopped and laid the pants down on her bed. She sat down because she knew something wasn't right. Taking a deep breath, she leaned back on the bed and tried to pull her phone out of her pocket. "Oh God," she groaned, realizing that it was her ex Zeke that texted her. "Why can't he just leave me alone? He made my life a living nightmare and he still won't stop," She thought, looking up at the ceiling. She threw her phone down on the bed and ignored it. Natalie got up and started getting ready to go to her grandparents house, to their annual New Year's Eve party.

It wasn't a formal event, it was barely even organized, but she decided to dress nicely anyway. She looked in the closet and found a black velvet sweater. "This'll do," she thought as she threw it onto the nearby bed. She put on her white fluffy bathrobe and sat down at her vanity and she heard her phone buzz again. She sighed, with her cheeks puffing out to twice their size. "It's not gonna stop until I respond is it?" She thought, as she got up to get her phone. Her suspicions were correct, it was Zeke again.

"Please leave me alone," she texted.

"I just wanted to tell you happy new year and I'm sorry that you didn't get to spend it this year with Jason," he said.

Natalie was furious and wanted to pull her hair out. She wanted nothing more than for that psychopath to leave her alone. Still, she didn't let that get her down and she got dressed. "I'm not putting much makeup on," she said as she covered her face with powder and applied eyeliner and mascara. Natalie made her way back into the living room as she sat down on the couch and waited for the rest of her family to get ready.

She ignored the messages as best as she could, but they were still on the back of her mind. "I can't let this take over my night," she thought as she took a deep breath, calming herself down. She put her phone away, shoving as far down in her purse as she could and waited on her parents to get ready.

"It's about time!" She screamed as her sister walked into the living room.

"Oh hush," Kelcie responded, making Natalie burst into a chuckle.

She left the house, heading to her grandparents house, it was a New Years tradition in her family to celebrate there. The coming in of the new year 2019 felt amazing to those who were around her. Natalie was excited to see her family and celebrate. The bright holiday lights started to shine through the car windows, as she pulled up into the driveway, it gave her a euphoric sensation as she stepped outside to see them with her own eyes.

 Natalie walked up to the front door, and was invited in to see everyone gathered around tables, drinking punch and playing cards.

"Hey Natalie!" A voice came from another room. It was a cousin of hers that came from another room.

"Hi, everyone!" Natalie said excitedly. She walked over to the table where everyone was playing cards.

 In the middle of the card game, Natalie's phone buzzed. Not thinking anything of it, she briefly looked at her phone and realized that there was a Facebook message from someone named Matthew. "You're the woman of my dreams." The message said. Leaving Natalie feeling distraught. One of Natalie's family members saw that she was in distress, though she tried to hide it as best she could.

"What's wrong, Natalie?" Her aunt asked.

"I just keep getting messages from men telling me that I'm the woman of their dreams without them even meeting me." Natalie said, sounding defeated.

"You should respond back and tell him that you're the man of my nightmares." The aunt responded back, making Natalie chuckle and feel better.

The night progressed on, and it was a great evening. The party was great, the ball dropped and all were preparing to leave and go home. Natalie and her sister prepared to leave, when the phone buzzed again. Natalie ignored it this time around, deciding that it was best to wait until she got home to check the notification.

Natalie made it home at two o'clock in the morning. She quickly washed her hair, face and changed into pjs, leaving her phone on her bed. Leaving the bathroom and entering into her bright pink bedroom, she noticed a notification on Twitter. Diana, was following her. Natalie's heart stopped, as she was taken aback by what was happening. This insane woman was going to make her life a living nightmare. Natalie was fueled with anger, so much so that she was physically shaking. She was also only following Natalie, and no one else, clearly targeting her. Instantly, she took screen shot of the profile, and sent it to her sister, who was already sound asleep.

The next morning, Natalie arose to the sound of her sister complaining. This wasn't unusual, but this time it was different. Natalie looked at her phone that had a text message from Kelcie saying "wow".
"Can you believe she did that?" Kelcie was saying. "Delusional Diana's over here thinking her child is innocent."

Natalie got up and went into the living room to find her sister on the phone to her mother, who was at work that morning.

A week had passed and things had settled down a little bit. Natalie was back in a normal routine. That week, one of her father's longtime friends had passed away. On a rainy Friday evening, Natalie sat curled up on the couch with a blanket and her cat at her feet. Her parents were on their way home from work and she waited for them in the living room, because she knew that they were going to the viewing that evening. Natalie had already decided that she wasn't going to anymore funerals unless they were necessary.

Kelcie came in the front door, and threw her backpack on the floor.

"Well, you look comfortable," Kelcie said.

"I am comfortable," Natalie responded, laughing.

She came inside and changed clothes, and sat down in the red recliner near the front door. Natalie stared outside and the rain hitting the window, letting her thoughts take over her. "It's weird how they died at the exact same time," Natalie thought, knowing how superstitious people were around her.

Natalie sighed and got up off the couch to charge her phone, knowing that she was going to be gone for the rest of the night. She sat back down on the couch and forced herself to stay awake.

There were large crowds expected. The church pastor spoke with Natalie's father a few days before and requested that he be a gatekeeper. The night of the funeral, Natalie chose not to go. Instead Natalie chose to go visit with her grandparents. Funerals were hard for Natalie, it brought back too many memories that were still very fresh. It had only been a year since Jason died.

Kelcie also chose to go with Natalie, and their parents agreed.

"Jeff, why don't you and Kelcie go to town first? That way you can come straight home after the service is over,"

"We can do that," Kelcie said as she went to her room and changed her clothes.

Kelcie stood in the living room and waited for the rest to get ready. to town in separate vehicles and decided on the way where they were going to eat at, texting back and forth with Natalie. Eventually, the chose a quick fast food restaurant.

Kelcie and her father pulled into the restaurant parking lot first, when she noticed a vehicle that looked very familiar. "Oh my God, dad, I think that's Dustin!" Kelcie said.

"Are you sure?" He asked.

"Yeah, I'm pretty sure. I had better call Natalie and tell her, she may not want to be here with him in there," Kelcie said, as got her phone out of her sweatshirt pocket.

It was a gray truck ford truck, and they weren't exactly sure if it was him or not, until they looked inside and saw him sitting in a booth near the window. Once Kelcie got out of the car, she knew for a fact that it was Dustin. She saw the fire fighter sticker placed on the back windshield. Around that time, Natalie and her mother pulled in. Natalie decided that she still wanted to eat there. She was not going to let something like him ruin her life. She was tired of running from him. Natalie got out of her car, as Kelcie was calling Natalie to warn her.

"I'm here you don't you have to call," Natalie joked, as she declined the call.

Kelcie laughed as she put her phone away.

"Are you sure that eating here won't bother you?" She asked, just to make sure that Natalie was okay.

"Yeah, I'm absolutely fine, plus It hurts him more than it hurts me, and I'm not gonna let something like him stop me from enjoying myself," she said. Natalie chose to go there anyway. Natalie said in excitement. She finally did not live in fear of Dustin anymore.

Natalie stepped inside and as soon as Dustin noticed her, he began to sweat. "Oh my God, it's her," he thought, as she made her way to the counter. Dustin hid his face from her as best he could. Looking at his phone and not making eye contact with her, hoping that she would not notice him.

Natalie was little nervous about the reaction that she would get, but that soon turned into rage as she stepped inside the building. Dustin was sitting next to a window and did not realize Natalie at first. "I just want to hit him," her mother said.

"Not nearly as bad as I do," Natalie responded.

Dustin looked up and spotted her. He was stunned to see her, since he had not seen her in well over a year. Natalie rolled her eyes at him and looked away, but Dustin panicked. His face turned white and he started shaking. He hid behind his phone, trying to avoid any contact with Natalie.

"I guess he really is guilty," Natalie said, silently. "He can't even face me,"

Natalie finished her dinner and left the restaurant, laughing in the car at what just happened.

"I don't know, but I'm pretty sure that Dustin's guilty," Natalie's mother leaned in and said.

"Yeah, I would say so," Natalie said, feeling relieved at the closure that God had just given her. Natalie was on a high that she had not felt in a really long time

Chapter 12

The nasty weather had finally cleared and the floods of February dissipated, giving a new hope to those who were in the county. Natalie was sitting at home, alone, while everyone else was out with friends, having a good time. Natalie's depression had made a violent comeback. She had a depression relapse, sending her back to therapy and back on medication again. Her mind had time to roam, too much time. Things slowed down, having more time on her hands was terrible. She held her head in her hands and cried, "why can everyone else be happy, but I can't?" She questioned as she sat on the floor next to her bed, hiding.

Natalie made a lot of progress in her healing journey. She was making strides, but suddenly she began to feel stagnant. Her life was going nowhere and she was sliding into a deep depression again. Her PTSD flashbacks returned. She couldn't go one night without thinking about what happened to Jason. She missed him and felt anger. "I should have been married by now," Natalie thought, loosing hope in ever finding another partner and seriously considered staying alone for the rest of her life. every bit of it in an instant. "I've got to go back to therapy," she thought, tired of being harassed and humiliated by a family of sociopaths. It was taking a toll on her mentally and physically.

It was just a few weeks before her 24th birthday and she made the choice to go back to therapy. She didn't want to, but she thought she was loosing her mind. She made her appointment, depressed, disappointed and ashamed. "I thought this part of grief was supposed to be over now," she thought, controlling her emotions the best she could. She wanted to pull her hair out, gripping onto her red locks of hair and screaming.

"I'm 24 years old and I'm still single," she said, crying. Wondering why her life has been as bad as it was for so long. Being alone was not good for her. She wasn't a strong independent woman. Natalie simply just functioned better with someone by her side. "Maybe I'm too dependent on other people to make me happy," she thought, feeling like she was left all alone.

"Oh God, I really am alone," she thought, looking down at her hands. She started thinking dark thoughts. "I shouldn't be single. I'll never get married and I don't want to wait longer than two years," she thought as her breathing became constricted. Her heart rate increased, pounding harder with each breath she tried to take. She started to panic, and tears ran down her cheeks. "Satan leave me alone!" She screamed. Natalie couldn't breath anymore. Her chest hurt from trying to get a deep breath.

She regained her composure, with her head still reeling, she stood up and pulled herself together. She waited a few minutes until she was completely calm, then left the room. She got up off the floor and went to lay down on the couch. She was exhausted and weary, but she still had things to do. She laid back on the couch, crossing her feet and gave a sigh of relief. She looked up at the ceiling, examining her life from the beginning until now. "Lord, just take me already. I can't do this anymore," she begged. Suddenly her phone buzzed. "Who could that be?" She thought, as she rose up on the couch and got her phone. It was a message from one of Jason's friends. She sighed, because she didn't feel like talking, but responded anyway.

"Hey," she responded.

Natalie began to grow closer to Jason's best friend, Blake. The two had become like siblings over the course of Jason's death, leaning on one another to help them through their grief. A friend who understood her was what Natalie needed, and she took advantage of that. Blake visited with Natalie often, and one day in particular, he stopped out of the blue at her house.

They talked forever about life in general, then something else came up.

"You know, I saw the accident report. It was all made up crap," Blake said.

"I figured that. That's why I don't look at stuff like that. It just makes me mad," Natalie said.

"I know. I also know that Dustin's truck wasn't investigated by the state,"

"Yeah, I actually talked to the tow truck driver who took Jason's vehicle and apparently Paul Howard took his vehicle." Natalie explained.

"Words cannot describe how much I hate that bunch of people." Natalie said.

The subject of the conversation changed and went to talk about their lives and their friends lives.

"You know, Travis is gonna be a dad," Blake said.

Natalie paused before answering, "I don't want to hear things like that right now," Natalie said.

"I am so sorry," Blake assured as he tried to console Natalie

"It's okay. I'm just so tired of hearing about everyone getting everything I wanted. I may have a decent career, but what's the point if I'm still alone?" Natalie asked, feeling hopeless.

"So, Dustin called me the other day," he said.

"You're joking," Natalie said.

"No, I'm not joking. He called to tell me that he was thinking about proposing to his girlfriend,"

Natalie paused. Her worst fear was sitting there right in front of her face.

"I was so afraid of that happening," Natalie said, with tears in her eyes.

Natalie's parents finally made it home after giving her and Blake some time to talk. Blake stayed around and spoke to them for a few hours, before finally leaving. Natalie felt good being able to express how she felt to someone who was not part of her family. Though her soul was still troubled upon learning about Dustin wanting to get married.

"Why does he have the option to get married when he took mine away from me?" she asked God.

Anger and disgust filled Natalie. "I hope what he did to me, happens to him," she thought.

"Well, you know what they say. Karma is a dish best served cold," Blake told her, laughing.

Natalie smiled in agreement. She thought what she was feeling was wrong, but it was not. What she felt was totally normal. She wanted revenge, but that wasn't possible. The only thing she could do was pray for God to bring justice where it needed to be.
promoting her book on twitter, trying to build up an audience of readers that would be interested in reading her work.

Her mental state improved in the next few days, in the next few days. She felt a sense of ease and belonging, but things were so stagnant. Her book was about to hit the shelves in just a few days and she was nervous, knowing that her life was about to change completely. She mentally prepared herself for the negative response she would receive, that's just how people are here. She chose to ignore the thoughts, and embrace the exciting new path that she was about to start.

She began to change things on her own, and decided to try out a dating app. Her mind was more focused on meeting someone than anything else. She knew that she had to wait on God, but he wasn't moving fast enough. She got her phone and done some searching on the internet to see which would be the best fit for her. By this time, Natalie was so confused. "Is this person who God wants me to be with?" She thought, as she looked through the notifications on her phone. She messaged a few of them, but they never really clicked. Natalie sighed and turned her phone off. "Looking for someone is more stressful than I thought," she said, with her eyes filling up with tears.

Days went by and finally, Natalie's life wasn't stagnant anymore. Natalie was excited to see a new opportunity to promote her book. She took the opportunity, being interviewed by a newspaper was a huge deal to her. She debated on whether or not she should take the offer, but ultimately decided to do so.

    The next day, Natalie was up early and by herself. She was enjoying the beauty of the bright March morning sun shining through the glass doors. She was enjoying the serenity of the quietness, drinking a cold glass of ice water while looking at the dew on the grass. Her phone rang, grabbing her attention. "Hello," she answered.

"Do you care to drive up to town and get some of these papers for me," her mother asked.

Natalie froze, knowing that she was going to have to face her fear of driving.

"I mean, I don't want to, but I will. What time do I need to leave?" She asked.

"Right now,"

    Natalie went and got the keys off the rack in the utility room. She wanted to be able to start driving again, but she didn't expect it to be that soon. Natalie still had a horrible fear of driving that she wasn't able to shake. It stuck around for a lot longer than it should have. She walked outside and the closer to the car she got, the more her hart raced. Her palms were sweaty and thought of ways to get out of going. She opened the door and sat down in the drivers seat, rubbing her hands on the steering wheel. "I don't want to do this, she thought. She started the car and back out of the driveway.

The cars that would come up behind her made her anxiety shoot through the roof. She gripped onto steering wheel and held it tightly, looking into the rear view mirror. She took a deep breath, "if I'm going to live a normal life, I have to get used to this," she told herself, praying that she would make it to her destination quickly.

Natalie could no longer drive her car, It had too many memories attached to it. Every time she sat down inside of it, all she could think about was Jason. The smell, and how her car caused him to die. thought as she got inside of the car. Her father got in on the passengers side and rode with her.

Natalie made it to the church, and picked up the paperwork she needed. The drive home was smoother, there was no traffic going the other way. She relaxed a little bit, but still continued to go around Lick Creek. Natalie got home and she was relieved. She turned the car off and got out of the vehicle, feeling like she had made a pivotal change in her life. She was happy and felt like she could do anything at that point. However, that fear of driving was still there and probably wasn't going to go away anytime soon.

She ran into the house, as fast as she could, away from the car. She didn't want to look at it anymore, but the sense of independence she had was amazing. She gave a sigh of relief as she fell back into the couch, with her arms wide open. "Thank God I don't have to do that anymore," she said, as she chuckled. Her happiness was finally restored, an emotion that seemed foreign to her. Her life was slowly starting to become normal again. She got up off the couch and went back into her room, her safe place.

That evening, she was sitting alone in bed, occupying herself with other things and biblical studies when Natalie got a notification on her phone. She didn't pay any attention to it and continued to do her own thing, thinking it was an email or something else of even less importance. Natalie finished up her studies and laid back against the headboard of the bed. She checked her phone and her heart sank. The notification was that of a distant cousin to Natalie. She tried reaching out to her again through social media. "Dear

Lord," Natalie sighed. Out of curiosity, Natalie checked her profile out and saw the date "01/07/18" written in her bio. Natalie's heart raced at the sight of it, seeing the day Jason died was a painful reminder. She missed having them as friends, but she did what she felt like she had to do, and blocked her. Cutting her out of Natalie's life permanently. "I do not owe them anything. They failed me in my situation." Natalie thought. Absolutely nothing in her life was the same, but she was thankful for that.

Natalie took a lot of time adjusting to her new life, and it wasn't easy. Everyday was a new step, with new decisions presenting themselves. She never knew what the next day would hold, throwing her off guard because she couldn't plan anything.

"I just want things to smooth over," Natalie thought, as she was stretching out on the couch after a long hard day of working in her great grandparents house.

"My feet are killing me!" Natalie said

"Oh I know, I'm worn out," her father responded.

Natalie was tired of sitting in the living room and went to soak her aching feet. "This is where I'm supposed to be," she thought. Her life was progressing, and she was excited for what the future held. She was so full of hope, but still some worries were there.

Natalie was still dealing with pent up anger and frustrations, so she turned to writing to express her feelings. Every night, she worked some on her first book, pushing herself to reach her word goal. Letting these feelings out gave Natalie a brand new perspective on her life. "Maybe this isn't the end for me," she thought. Natalie no longer put up with things like she used to and was no longer codependent.

It was a bright sunny day in late March, Natalie was busy redecorating her new bedroom in her new home. She used her bedroom as an office. After a few hours of cleaning and reorganizing things, she stood back and looked at the room, being quite happy with how it turned out. "I think that's it for physical labor today!" She said, smiling as she left the room. Natalie flopped down on the couch, propped her feet up on the arm and took a deep breath to relax. Natalie pulled her phone out from her pocket and worked on some other projects that she had started. Including promoting her work to create a demand for it. Natalie was at home alone and she was expecting her sister to be home around 4:30 that evening.

Natalie heard a car pull into the driveway, she quickly got up, knowing that it was Kelcie who had just gotten home.

"Well, what did you learn today?" Natalie asked Kelcie, as soon as she stepped through the front door.

"Nothing," Kelcie responded, taking her shoes and backpack off. When her sister arrived home, who had just gotten home from beauty school, Natalie left her desk and came into the living room to have a conversation. She had decided to check her email. To Natalie's surprise, she had received an email from the Nonfiction Author's Association. It was specifically addressed to her with information about her account with them, which was extremely unusual because it was mostly updates about club meetings, discounts on marketing and ideas for writing other books. This time was different.

Natalie felt like giving up completely. She wanted to throw in the towel and just leave it alone. Kelcie soon interrupted her thoughts and suggested that they go to West Liberty.

Natalie liked that idea and got up to change her clothes. Getting out of the house for a minute is exactly what she needed. She put on a sweat shirt and a pair of jeans, and left her house. She held back her emotions, knowing that it would make it worse if she spoke about it and she didn't want to think about this. She put it in the back of her mind because no one understood her pain anyway and she put a smile on her face. She was determined to enjoy herself and get some good food.

The one person she could confide in was no longer here, and she was left alone. She had no friends or anyone she could open up to. Natalie turned and looked out the window, thinking about her life. Natalie was so desperate for a friend. She missed her old life and longed for it to come back. She spent hours upon hours praying to God that things would change.

It was just at the turn of summer. The weather was heating up, and the sun became brighter. Natalie's life and career was heading in a great direction, but there was still something didn't feel right. Natalie's Spirit was troubled, knowing that things were too good to be true. However, she wrote it off as an attack from Satan and not a warning from God. She shook it off and came into the living room, dressed and ready to do some small things around the house. Painting was something Natalie loathed, but she had no choice.

"We've been here for months now, why didn't we just finish the painting before we moved in?" Natalie complained.

"We just got behind," her father responded as Natalie was digging through the living room closet to find the can of white paint.

Natalie found the can underneath a small latter that Jason had bought her father as a Christmas present. Her grandmother, who loved nothing more than doing home projects, was called into help. They jokingly called her The Kraken, because no matter what was going on, things had to be done. The first task for Natalie that week was painting, but she didn't really feel like doing anything. Around this time, Natalie had fallen back into a deep depression. She was back on her medication and in her mind was taking steps backwards in life.

Every single day, Natalie struggled. Her life was meaningless. "I went through all that torture, and what do I have to show for it?" Natalie questioned, as she changed her clothes and prepared for the day. She stood back and sighed, whining, because she just wanted to stay in bed. "Maybe this will be good for me," she thought as she laced to her tennis shoes. Natalie came into the living room, where her sister was sitting on the couch, planning on going to meet with some friends, instead of helping.

Natalie was furious. No matter the day or time, every time The Kraken showed up, She was always the one left to do the work.

"Are you ever going to do anything?" Natalie asked.

"I can't help it, mamaw never comes on days that I want,"

"That doesn't matter, you're home today, you don't have to get on the road every time you're home," Natalie screamed as she slammed the door. Still fuming, she got inside the truck and rode up the road to the work site

Natalie was so depressed, and did not feel like doing much of anything, yet time after time, she was always expected to do something. It wasn't her family's fault. They don't understand what depression is, though she expressed this to them several times, they either didn't listen or they just didn't understand. Natalie dipped her brush in the bucket of wood stain, and rolled a coat on the boards.

"I hate my life so bad," she thought, wanting to die as she finished up working on her old home. She came home, covered in sweat. She ran to her room, and took a shower as fast as she could, knowing that she was too filthy to sit down on her couch. "Oh Lord, there's more to do tomorrow," she said as she turned on the shower.

Kelcie was actually going to be home the next day, making Natalie's anger subside. She didn't have to be there all the time, but leaving every single time something needed to be done was torture. They were working in the kitchen, painting an antique door that they had taken from the old house. It had been stores in the barn for a while, and they chose to use it.

The next morning came early, and once again, they were at it. Natalie's depression was significantly better today. The sun was bright and this was something that she wanted done for a long time. She wedges herself in the utility room where her sister and her grandmother were at.

"Hey Kelso, scoot the paint bucket over here towards me," Natalie said, as she was a wet paint brush before completely submerging it in paint.

"Here you go!" Kelcie said, pushing the bucket towards her on the kitchen floor.

"Thank you!" She said, in a joking manner, stumbling over the paint bucket and catching herself on the dryer. Laughter erupted from behind her and she couldn't contain herself either. She calmed down and dipped her brush into the paint, brushing it onto the door.

"You all aren't doing a real good job painting there girls. Look at that Natalie, You've missed a spot,"

Natalie laid her wet brush down over the opened can of white paint and said "I'll tell you what, if you think you can do it better, why don't you just get up and do it yourself?"

"No, I can't do that now,"

"Beggars can't be choosers!" Kelcie screamed, at their father said, sitting in a chair at the kitchen table watching them.

This was how Natalie was spending most of her days now. "Why, God, did you make me from go from getting married to doing chores like a child again?" She thought. She was so unhappy with her life, everything was pointless. She wasn't working towards bettering herself anymore, she was just doing small house renovations in preparation for guests to come and visit or other reasons that don't matter much. Now all she had to look forward to was spending time with her family, and even that was getting old.

Her book was written and published, and the release day was approaching soon. She was excited, but still depressed. Even happy things made her sad. She was nervous, but excited to finally have a goal set in planning on having a book signing. Natalie had been working on that for a while, she had everything ready to go except for a location to have it. She spent hours searching around the internet for venues. Originally, she wanted to have it the church. It was in a location that easily accessible and right in the middle of town. It was perfect, until she spoke to the preacher about it who couldn't allow it due to the rules. Natalie was okay with that, she had no problem with finding someone else. A friend of hers that went to church with her recommended the local library.

Natalie's eyes lit up with excitement, because that was even better than the church, she just hadn't thought of it. She gave him the go ahead and went on about her business.. A good word was put in for her and she waited a while before finally making plans.

"My phone is ringing." Natalie said. She stoped painting and answered the phone.

"Hello" she said.

"Hi, I'm calling about scheduling your book signing. When were you thinking? "

"Great, I was thinking about the 25th of May or the first of June if possible." Natalie said.

Natalie was elated. She liked the attention she was getting, though she hated to admit that. Natalie was not one to brag about herself. Pride was something that she was afraid of, but she was definitely proud of herself with this achievement. It was a call from the library to schedule her book signing. She stepped outside to take the call, since her house was a complete dead zone. at the local Magoffin County Library. June was just a couple of days away, and Natalie had originally scheduled the signing for the 25th of May. She rescheduled for the 8th of June when her family members bought all of her books at the family reunion.

Natalie was ready for the book signing. She spent the rest of that night looking at things to entertain the guests. She started planning as soon as she was given the go ahead. She picked out everything from

Bookmarks to tablecloths, and made an appointment to go meet with the library director the next day. She had to, in order to get everything ready.

The next day, noon came around. Natalie got up out of bed and quickly changed into professional clothing. Her father drove her to town, since Natalie still had a horrible fear of driving.

"Hi, I'm here to speak to melody, is she here?" Natalie asked.

"She's here Melody!" The receptionist screamed from her desk across the room. Natalie stood there, looking at her phone and waited for a few moments. She did not know where to go or what to do. Feeling awkward, She stood over by the window. After five minutes of awkward silence, eventually she came out of the back room.

"Hi there! Come on into my office," she said as she was looking through a stack of papers.

"Okay!" Natalie said, breathing a sigh of relief. She put her phone up and followed her down a long hallway to very small, outdated office. Melody sat down at her desk and got a planner out of a filing cabinet.

"So when are we talking about?" Melody asked.

"I was thinking around the end of May to the middle of June." Natalie responded. "I know I originally said the 25th, and I hate to change on such short notice, but I was thinking around the 15th of June."

They spoke for a few moments, not about the book, but about Jason and his influence in the community.

"Jason was such a good man." Melody said. "He'd be very proud of you if he was still here."

"I know. He touched everyone's life in some way." Natalie said, wishing he was still here. Everyone loved him, but Natalie loved him more than everyone else. Everywhere he went lives were touched. Reminiscing about Jason made Natalie miss him. She missed him so much, even though it had been over a year since he died. "I wish he could be here to celebrate this with me. I wish I had someone to celebrate this with me." Natalie thought.

Natalie stayed and talked for a while, planning her book signing. When she left the library, she was in good spirits. Excited for what was to come in the next couple of weeks. She planned for her book signing and promoted it on social media. The entire town was excited, except for Diana and her family. It actually came as a shock to them, especially Diana. Diana thought she stopped the book, that she had won the battle and shut Natalie up for good. Needless to say, she was furious and embarrassed. The only thing she knew to do was torment. Diana's daughter, found the Facebook post and began to mock Natalie. Telling the world that she was only doing this for money and calling her a liar.

The next morning. Natalie was up early. She barely slept out of anger and frustration. She tried to get some sleep, but that was interrupted by a text message from her mother. "Delusional Diana is at it again," It said, "Oh Lord," Natalie thought, before evening opening the notification. She saw that it contained a picture, nervous, she opened it. It was a screen shot of comment that Diana had left on a post of hers from a couple of months back.

"What her mother is implying is that there are things in this that are not true. I'd like to know what those are. What she put on the website was simply not true. I have pictures, but I won't stoop to that level. I am glad that she is writing about their lives. I'll have to get one and read it."

Natalie has no words to say. She chose to turn the other cheek and ignore it, because that hurt them more than anything. Anything Natalie did, she watched like a hawk. Any chance they had to sue her, they would have, but Natalie was a relatively quiet person anyway. Natalie wanted to stand up for herself, but her hands were tied.

Natalie was humiliated. "I can take this stuff, but I prefer to keep it to myself," She said. Natalie was depressed from humiliation to the point where she refused to leave the house. Her parents would not let her leave the house by herself, in fear that she would get jumped or attacked.

Days passed by and Natalie's life got smoother. Things had calmed down and Natalie relaxed. One afternoon, Kelcie was at work. She had a part time job at the local grocery store that she kept around just for extra money, since Kelcie spent most of her days at beauty school. To balance out her work load, she only worked on the weekends. It was a slow Saturday in the store. Only a few customers showed up the entire day, so they decided to shut down the store early. It was almost closing time, and Kelcie was getting things in order to close. As she was checking out her last customer, and getting cleaning supplies to clean her station, she noticed that Diana was waiting for line to clear out. Diana singled her out, just so she could aggravate Kelcie.

"Oh my God," Kelcie whispered under her breath.

"Well, hi there! How are you?" Diana asked, in a sickening tone, obvious as to what she was doing.

"I'm great, how are you?" Kelcie responded, rolling her eyes so hard that it caused pain in her forehead.

"Are these on digital?" she asked, still trying to make Kelcie day something.

After Diana left, Kelcie grabbed her phone and ran outside to call Natalie.

"You're never gonna guess who just came through my checkout line," Kelcie said.

"Who was it?" Natalie asked.

"Delusional Diana, and she had the most sickening tone to her voice," Kelcie implied.

"What did you do?"

"Well, I was just as sickening back to her. Ain't nobody gonna out butt kiss me!"

Natalie and Kelcie laughed off the experience. Thinking that this would be a one time thing. Unfortunately, it kept happening to Kelcie. Week after week. Diana knew her schedule from watching Kelcie so much. With this stalking happening, Natalie's family recommended that she not leave the house alone. Natalie, being small in stature, was in danger. The senile old woman, probably was not too much of a threat, but Diana obviously had mental issues.

Natalie knew that leaving her home alone was a part of her daily life. So, she got a derringer and carried it with her everywhere she went. and Jason had one together, and since he was gone, the dog was too.

Chapter 13

Thunder rolled in the distance as the wind began to pick up. A strong cool breeze rushed through the field behind her house. The sky darkened with gray storm clouds, as they moved in closer and closer from behind the mountains. Natalie watched the sky turn before her eyes. To her, it was beautiful. Her eyes riveted towards the sky, she watched as rain began to fall as the wind blew her hair, forcing her to go back inside the house. It was noon, and the house was pitch black. She flipped a light switch, turning on the kitchen light and went to the back door, standing with her face pressed against the glass, watching the storm, amazed by God's incredible power.

"Get away from that window, you'll get struck by lightning," her father yelled from the living room.

Natalie laughed and backed away, easing her fathers' mind. She came back into the living room and sat down in the recliner, checking the weather forecast.

"A severe thunderstorm," Natalie said out loud without realizing. It was giving a high chance of rain. Natalie looked out the window, amazed by the storm clouds and God's magnificent power. Her cat came over and sat in her lap, watching the storm with her.

"Natalie, do you want to go town with me? It'll get you out the house for a little while?" Natalie's father asked. Natalie turned around and said "Yeah, I guess. I don't have anything else to do." She responded

"Do you think we can beat the rain?" She asked.

"Yeah, we'll be alright," Her father assured. Natalie grabbed her raincoat and an umbrella just in case. "Why do you have that for?" Her father asked.

"Anything can happen." Natalie said. Natalie got inside the gray truck and noticed small raindrops hitting the windows of her Father's pickup truck. Natalie smiled, being thankful that she was prepared. Friday afternoon. Natalie and her father were headed to town to a farmers market that was only supposed to be opened for just that day. Natalie was tired, but she chose to go anyway. It was under a tent in front of a Baptist church on the main road. The rain had subsided by the time they arrived.

Her father parked his truck behind the church where everyone else seemed to be going. The parking lot was full, most of which were older women, making Natalie feel uncomfortable. The older women were standing outside of their vehicles, and having a conversation. Natalie felt out of place by her presence. She felt like she was the focal point among the women. Her anxiety kicked in and her mind told her that they were judging her, but in reality that probably was not the case. Natalie made her way through the crowd of women, trying to get what they were actually there for, corn.

The old man who owned the shop, Mr. Porter, was sitting in a chair that was next to his truck bed, that was filled with ears of corn. Natalie's father was intrigued by the price and went over to look around and he started talking to Mr. Porter. Natalie was looking at flowers, when she was noticed by him and he spoke up.

"Is that your daughter?" He asked.

"Yeah, that's mine." Her father answered back.

"Let me ask you son, do you take that girl to church?" Mr. Porter said to Natalie's father.

"Yes sir, I do, every Sunday." Natalie's father responded while shaking Mr. Porter's hand proudly.

"That's how you're supposed to raise a child." Mr. porter said, not realizing that Natalie was in her mind twenties.

Natalie's father spoke with Mr. Porter some more and learned that he was a preacher at another local church, while Natalie was busy filling baskets with corn that her father had purchased. Four dozen he paid for. Natalie brought the baskets over to Mr. Porter so he could weigh them. He smiled at her and said "I heard corn adds more freckles." He said jokingly.

"I definitely don't need anymore of those." Natalie responded in a light hearted manner.

"Sissy, are you married?" He asked, genuinely concerned and her father spoke up from the side.

"Well" he said and paused for a moment. "It's been kind of a tragic story. She was supposed to get married, but her fiancé was killed in a car wreck last year."

"I hate to hear that, but there's one thing I can promise you, that if it's the Lord's will for you to be married, it will surely happen." Mr. Porter said, smiling, talking about how good of a man he heard Jason was. Natalie smiled, taking it as a sign from God.

The rain began to pour, making Natalie run towards the truck. She slammed the door and started thinking "what if it isn't God's will for me to be married?" She thought. Her heart almost stopped in her chest, realizing that she could be single for the rest of her life. Fear paralyzed her, but she tried not to think about it. She was jolted back into reality by a loud sound in the back end of the truck.

Her heart pounding, she turned around to see her father laughing as he threw bags of corn into the back of the truck. Natalie couldn't help but laugh as well. On the way home, she thought about that odd experience and again on how she could possibly be single for the rest of her life. "How do I know what God's will is for my life?" She pondered, watching the rain hit the window. Her mind kept going back and forth between believing that it was a sign from God for this man to show up in a time that she needed it the most, and the worst thing she could possibly imagine. Instead of her faith growing that evening, she became a victim of fear and fell into her emotions.

Natalie came home, and instantly ran towards the kitchen. She hadn't eaten all day, and lunch seemed like a great idea. "Why is it so cold in here?" She asked, getting a pot out from underneath the kitchen sink. "It's hot outside," her father responded.

Natalie ate and got sleepy, so she went to her room. On her night stand was a candle, she lit it and laid down. As soon as her head hit the pillow, her mind started racing. She couldn't hold the tears back anymore. She started sobbing, as it just a few months over the one year anniversary of Jason's death and her wounds were still not completely healed.

Natalie desperately wanted things to change. "I shouldn't even have to be looking for another man," Natalie thought, angered at the situation. The encounter with Mr. Porter made Natalie reassess her life, putting things into a perspective that didn't need to be there. "It's just Satan," she tried telling herself, but ultimately ended up crying herself to sleep.

Absolutely nothing in her life was the same, including her personality. She had changed in a way that was beneficial to her and people noticed it. When the beginning of summer of came, Natalie made the decision to move forward and that it was time to start dating again. She approached the dating scene slowly, not wanting to get into anything that wasn't going to lead into what she desired. Marriage. Natalie had became very levelheaded and could manage her emotions as if nothing had ever happened to her. She was, what some people claimed, back to "normal", but it was a new normal. Not only did things change for Natalie, but Natalie herself had changed. She was different and things that she used to put with was no longer an issue for her. She stopped hanging around people who didn't have good intentions.

Along with the new changes that came, a new set of problems also arose. Natalie became worried about her situation of being alone. No matter how much people tried to comfort her, telling her that there was no need to worry, it did not help her. Natalie remembered how God had spoken to her about dating, making her more frustrated that he had still not spoken to her to confirm her husband, even though she had been in the presence of many men. She tried to keep her spirits up, by trusting that He had already chosen someone for her. and when that man entered into her life, God would speak to her. She trusted what was spoken to her, three times. Each by several different people, confirming what she already knew. Thus came the attention of men. Natalie made a bold decision and started to put herself out there again. The attention that she got was something that she never expected to get. The newfound attention made her anxiety go through the roof. She felt unbelievably uncomfortable with all the comments she was getting.

"Why don't you come over to my house and swim, so I can see you in a bikini." One man shouted at her from afar, from a man who was sixteen years her senior. The thoughts of being with someone like that made her nauseous.

The next morning, Natalie went to go talk to her therapist, once again. She had gone a while without having to go see the therapist, but life had become too much to bare. She got ready in a hurry, almost tripping over things in her bedroom floor, since she slept later than her normal time. "Oh God, I'm gonna be late." She said out loud, throwing things together.

Natalie finally arrived at the therapist office and sat down.

"It's like Jason dies and I become the most attractive woman on this planet," Natalie said to her to her therapist.

"Well, you are very beautiful, so I can see why men would reach out to you. Have you tried taking time off social media?" she asked.

"I have. I don't know if I can do it though," Natalie stated

"I would suggest taking some time off of social media. It would do you some good. Social media makes everything worse than what it actually is,"

Something instantly clicked in Natalie's head. She agreed to the challenge, excited to actually spend time focusing on herself. "I really need a break." She thought. Taking a break was what she did. She slowly started distancing herself from social media. Nothing really interested her anyway. She did not care about what was going on in other people's lives and she did not care if people knew what was going on in her life.

A few weeks after banning herself from Facebook, and the withdrawal symptoms in the past. Natalie noticed that she was extremely relaxed. Keeping those things out of her sight made her feel better about herself. Natalie's confidence boosted and she wasn't as depressed as before. "Taking a break has been, by far, the best decision I've ever made," she said. because she did not have to worry about being behind.

Chapter 14

The leaves on the trees were turning orange and leaves were flying through the crisp fall air. Fall was one of the most beautiful times in the mountains of eastern Kentucky and it was Natalie's favorite time of the year. Jason's birthday was approaching, and Natalie was doing anything she could to not focus on it. Her grandmother was coming to visit her that day, and Natalie was excited to be able to have a conversation with someone that was not in her immediate family. "Hi mamaw," Natalie said, waving her hand up at her.

Natalie was feeling better, enjoying her time. She was realizing the change of the season. Fall is her favorite time of the year. She looked forward to decorating, cold weather and the seasons to come. Natalie was happy at those thoughts, excited that she had something to look forward to and occupy her time. Though Natalie was happy with the thoughts of seasonal change, but thoughts of being alone were dominant.

One evening, Natalie chose to go out shopping with her mother and her sister, spending time with both of them. Natalie was feeling particularly depressed that day. The thoughts of being alone one more second drove her insane. Knowing that she shouldn't be alone made her depression worse. Every day, Natalie looked at the calendar with disgust. "Another year single." She sighed, yearning to find love. She pleaded with God not to allow her to be single for two years, but it looked like it was going to happen that way.

Walking through the store was torment. Everywhere she looked, there were couples or images of people, who were younger than her, getting married. "Why can't I have that?" She thought as she stood and looked at the counter. It was on magazines, television, and just regular stock photos in picture frames. "Why are all these people getting married and I'm not?" She thought. Angry that she was still single, she tried to focus on other things. She didn't speak the rest of the time in the store, because if she did, she would have cried.

"Natalie, what's wrong?" Her mother asked.

"Nothing, there's just too many people in here," She lied , trying to avoid having a conversation and actually explaining what was wrong.

People who were married did not understand Natalie's situation and the advice that they would often give her was not very helpful, only making Natalie feel worse than before.

"Oh my God, I'm wasting my life." Natalie was thinking on the inside. She felt like there would be no end in sight to the suffering. All of her high school friends were married. looked back at the days she had wasted alone. Natalie had been single for well over a year, and needless to say, she was lonely. Twenty four years of age and still not married, something that was very uncommon in rural areas of Kentucky. Most people in that neck of the woods are married at eighteen, some sixteen, and definitely no later than twenty. Natalie spent too many hours of the day focused on her singleness, worried that she will forever be alone, causing intense depression.

Natalie stepped outside to get a fresh breath of air, staring up at the heavens, believing that God had failed her. Her breakthrough was prophesied over her, in seven days, her breakthrough was supposed to happen and it did not. She had gotten her hopes up, only be let down one more time. "Lord, why have you let me down again?" Natalie asked, trying her hardest not to cry.

Natalie could not date just anyone she wanted. God spoke to her on three separate occasions, the first being through a dream, the second through a prophetic word at church and the third through a friend of hers. She accepted this fact and truly wanted God to have a say in this matter. Having faith like that was difficult, especially when no one around her seemed to accept or believe the fact that the Lord has spoken to her and she has chosen to wait on God to speak to her about a man. Advice was coming from all angles of her life "why don't you date this person?" "Why are you still alone?" "Do you ever plan to get married?" and when Natalie answered telling them about what God had said her, they stared at her blankly in confusion.

Natalie was quite a beautiful woman. She just didn't see it. Jason reminded her of her beauty daily, and even then she still could not see her beauty on both the inside and out. Everywhere she went, she attracted men of all ages, young and old. Sometimes she was flattered by it, but more often, it became too much to handle and was extremely hard to deal with. It became a burden having men beg to be with her, even after turning them down, they tried to convince her otherwise. Date after date, she turned down. Some of the men did not take no for an answer. If Natalie did not want to go on a date or was not attracted to that man, then she would be called every bad name they could think of. A clear sign from God that those men were not the men she was supposed to be with. "Sometimes too much attention is a bad thing," Natalie thought.

Natalie became so frustrated with the attention she got. "I shouldn't be complaining, but I hate this so much. Why is it only men that are trash who are reaching out to me?" She thought. Men she was interested in were not interested in her, and the men she was not interested in was doing everything they could to try and get with her.

One afternoon, Natalie was relaxing. Trying to take her mind off of the stressful day she had. She got tired of getting all of the internet attention she was receiving, so she decided to take a social media break for a while. She started her break and felt amazing. The greatest few weeks she had felt in her life. The break allowed her to focus on her career and God, giving her a sense of direction in her life. Even though she had her sense of direction back, Natalie was still lonely. She made an appointment with her therapist. The first time she had to go back in months, to help control her depression.

Natalie's loneliness grew too much to bare, she longed for a husband and even just some friends to the point that she cried herself to sleep at night. Wondering why God has left her out of so much. The friends that Natalie did have were always busy, gone or completely unreliable to her. Most of them were married and had children, she did not understand what that was like and that's all they talked about, depressing her worse than before. She had a taste of freedom, but then that freedom was taken away from her at the hands of someone else. The adjustment was hard, and the lack of help she had was harder.

One cool fall evening, Natalie was at home alone. Her parents were gone to Lexington and her sister was at beauty school. The silence in the house made Natalie even more lonesome, giving her time to think and reflect on her life. Natalie sat down in the brown fluffy recliner next to the door.

"Lord, Give me some kind direction. I have no idea where my life is headed. I feel like I'm walking in the dark and have no where to go." Natalie said, beginning to cry and trying to deal with her anxiety.

"When Lord? When will the misery end? When will I receive my breakthrough?" She cried. Not only did Natalie want to know when it was going to happen, but she also wanted to know who she was meant to be with. The intense confusion lead Natalie into a deep depression, so much so that she had to go back on her medication. hat had come upon her. She was interested in someone, but would he want to be with her? The questions that Natalie dealt with were terrible and had effects that were detrimental to her mental and physical health.

The next Sunday morning at exactly seven o'clock in the morning, Natalie was awakened out of a deep sleep by a loud voice saying "Testimony". Natalie sprung up in bed, rubbing her eyes. "What was that?" Natalie asked. her head spinning and not quite sure what was going on. She sat there for a moment, letting the moment sink in for a moment, before lifting her hands in praise. She was so excited by what has happened, that she struggled to go back to sleep before church. She finally did, and gained an extra hour of sleep.

Natalie's life changed in that moment on that bright Sunday morning. She was happy and wanted to tell everyone about the encounter that she had. Natalie woke up around nine, her cat prancing around her head in the bed, trying to look out the window. "What are you doing Bud?" She asked as she stroked his black fur. She got up out of the bed, taking the cat with her.

Her life did not get worse, but her situation did. Each day, Natalie would wake up and feel mental pressure like never before. She longed for a husband every day, and she just because she didn't have one. Her family and friends just couldn't feel the void anymore. No one could feel the void, including God. She loved the Lord and spent time with him every day, but she needed human touch.

"What are you in such a good mood for?" Natalie's mother asked.

"I just slept good last night." Natalie said, keeping her words from God to herself.

Natalie prayed for a long time and for the first time, she saw hope that day. Her faith grew and she truly believed God for a husband. Natalie was hopeful that week. "Maybe I'll finally get my blessing." She thought. yet she was left empty handed each time she got her hopes up. She would take one step forward and three steps backwards. Then finally, her perspective changed and supernatural faith came to her. She knew things were changing in her favor.

Natalie's happiness was overflowing. Changes brought on new challenges. She was finally becoming content with her life, and praising God for what she did have, instead of what she did not have. Sunday evening Natalie was in the shower, washing away the stress of the day. Suddenly, Natalie heard her phone buzz against the marble vanity top in the bathroom. Out of curiosity, she pulled the curtain back and looked at her phone. "Oh My God." She sighed. It was a message from an old high school friend, who was crushing on her since she was fourteen years old. Being the person that she is, Natalie responded back. The conversation was normal at the beginning. He asked her about how her life was going and so forth. Then, one message sent the conversation astray. "I had a dream about us dancing under the stars last night, and there was a man there, I don't know who he was, but he said he wanted us to be together." The message read. Natalie instantly knew that he was sending subliminal messages about Jason, and he just would not come out and say it. "Oh my God, he's already in a relationship with someone, but he still wants to be with me." She thought. was trying to convince her that Jason appeared to him in a dream and told him that he was supposed to be with her. Natalie looked at her phone and breathed in anger.

"Why would he say something like this to me?" Natalie pondered. It took her a while to respond. She knew that

God was going to speak to her when she met her husband, so she did not fall for the claims. It just made her sad that people would go to such extreme lengths to try to be with her.

Natalie began taking these things as a sign, and she got excited. Really excited. Knowing that her prayer was about to be answered. A friend of hers told her to stay busy until God moved in her life, so to keep herself busy, she scheduled several book signings, since she did not get to have one. This time, extra planning went into finding places to have one. She made it a personal goal to distance herself as far away from the county as she possibly could. "I don't need them to be successful," She thought. once and for all. Though Natalie's joy was soon met with opposition. Her first book signing was at the Kentucky Apple Festival. She sat up her booth both days, Friday and Saturday.

That Friday morning was a chilly one. The temperature was slightly below average and could be felt throughout the house. Natalie's alarm was set for 6 am, but awoke five minutes early. Natalie curled back up under the blankets for warmth, trying to stay awake. struggled to see, because it was still pitch black outside. All of a sudden, Natalie heard her door creek open. "Get up Natalie, it's time to go!" Her father screamed, as he peeked his head into the dark room.
"Do I have to?" she groaned.
"Yeah, I'd reckon you do," he said.

She got up and stumbled around until she found the light switch. "Oh that's bright," Natalie said as she flipped the switch. She rubbed her eyes and slowly got dressed before she took the braids out of her hair. Natalie was having second thoughts as she came into the living room with her box of books and other things. "I don't know if I want to do this or not," she thought as she sat the box down for her father to carry outside. "Is this everything?" Her father asked.

"Yeah, that's it," she replied as she left the room to go apply her makeup. She looked at the dark circles underneath her eyes and worried as she plunders through her vanity drawers to find the best concealer she had.

Natalie was tired, but she was so excited. So many people were depending on her to have a book signing, and people lost faith in her because it fell through. This was her chance to finally redeem herself. She finally had the opportunity to be able to sign her work and share her story with others. She was proud of herself and talked herself up in the mirror before she left. She was nervous too. Being in front of people was something that Natalie was never good at. She had intense social anxiety. Jason tried to help her through it, but it didn't help. The more people who knew about her, knew about her story. It was better for her career wise, but she knew that getting her story out there and spreading her story to the world would help others who are going through similar situations.

Natalie left the house in good spirits. She was ready and her exhaustion was replaced with excitement. She stopped by her grandmother's house to pick her up.
"Are you sure you brought enough books?" Her father asked.
"Yeah, I'm sure. I didn't want to bring too many or else I would've been carrying a lot back home," she replied.
"If you say so,"

Throughout the course of the two days, Natalie spoke to many people who had also lost loved ones. One in particular who had lost her daughter.
"Did you write the book?" The dark haired woman asked.
"Yes, I did." Natalie responded.

"I lost my daughter recently and I've had a really hard time dealing with it."

Natalie offered her condolences to the grieving woman, and signed the book for her. Natalie's heart filled with joy, knowing that God was using her to help others in similar situations. "This is why you brought me here." She smiled as she spoke to God.

Throughout the day Natalie saw many people she knew. One of them was a close friend of her grandfather and a member of the church Natalie and Jason used to attend frequently together.

"Hi! He said when he spotted her.

"Let me give you a hug!" He screamed, running over to her to hug her as tight as he could.

"How have you been?" He asked.

"Good. Really good." Natalie responded.

"You know, you may have went through that, but your life has went up tremendously. He's still with you, and you keep going up." Jim said.

The next day, Natalie slept in an hour later. Instead of waking up at six, she woke up at seven. Daylight was breaking, and she was relieved because she was not rushed. She also planned ahead and the night before, she laid out, hanging them on the back of her closet door.
"Is your Mamaw coming with you all?" Natalie's mother asked.
"No, it's just me and Dad," she said.
"Oh okay, I will be over there later. I want to wait on Kelcie to get out of the bed first,"

Natalie agreed and loaded up her stuff in the back of her fathers pick up truck. Natalie arrived back at her station around ten o'clock that morning. All of her stuff was still where she left it, making setting up a lot easier. Traffic was slow, since it was the second day and most people were there looking for things on sale.

Throughout the day, Natalie sold a total of twelve

books, so she decided to finish up early, being satisfied

with her work. As she was finishing up her work and

talking to some of her friends from church.

Chapter 15

Natalie's days were now filled with contentment. She was finally at a point where she was happy, caused by a new chapter in her life. She was focusing on herself and making sure she was okay before anything else. Her mind and her body was her main priority.

Natalie stopped worrying, because God told her that she would be married. However, she did not knew when.

Everyday, she was spending more time with God. The presence of God was so strong around her, and she was at peace. So much peace that one evening, she took a nap. She drifted off into a deep sleep, and was awakened by her repeating "Abba Shalom," At first, she thought it was just her mind replying what she heard at church about Absalom, King Solomon's brother. Upon further searching, it meant Father of Peace.

Natalie's life was totally different. Absolutely nothing was the same and her life was still changing for the better.

By the month of October, Natalie felt a shift in her soul. It was different from anything that she had ever felt before. She could not explain why or what this feeling was. Though, she knew this was exactly what she needed. Natalie was finally prepared for marriage. She started submitting herself to God, and getting rid of the anger and bitterness she had held onto for the past two years.

Natalie's career as an author was going well. She started to bring herself out of debt and was planning on buying herself a new car. But no matter how many things she had been blessed with, she was still sad and depressed. Natalie couldn't be happy, but she wanted to be. The depression kept lingering over her, and if anything, got worse. Natalie still had issues with anger that she felt was holding her back from moving into new positions.

"I need to get over this," She said. "I cannot keep living my life base on other people's opinions and with these crazy people trying to ruin my life,"

"Have you tried getting a restraining order?" The therapist asked. Natalie said, sounding defeated.

Natalie struggled daily with the feeling of defeat and loneliness. Being twenty four years old and still single was hard. Though Natalie had been given many blessings, she was still missing something. All the success in the world couldn't fill the void of being alone.

"Why don't you talk to your friend?" The therapist suggested.

"You mean Blake?" She asked, in confusion.

"Yeah, I think it would be good for you to be less isolated and have someone to talk to." She responded.

Natalie thought about it for a moment and agreed. She was depressed and needed some form of a human connection. She couldn't eat or sleep for weeks. She would get hungry, but turn away from any food that was placed in front of her. When she would try sleeping, she couldn't. Trauma nightmares filled her mind. Dreams of Jason's body, death and burial were constantly taking over her life from PTSD. The therapist suggested that she be treated with the same medication that war veterans were treated with.

Natalie was cautious of taking the medicine. Being on blood pressure medicine for something other than high blood pressure was not an ideal situation. Natalie's parents were against the idea as well, so they decided to wait and see if they got better before going to that length.

The next day after therapy, Natalie reached out to Blake, and got no response. That was normal. He was a busy man, and she respected that. So Natalie found things to do to keep herself occupied. Though, no matter how occupied she was. The loneliness was still on the back of her mind.

Natalie's life started to take a drastic turn by the end of the month. Something happened inside of Natalie that she couldn't explain. Everything felt and looked different, but a good different. She had this huge shift that took place in her that she couldn't explain. Keeping the shift to herself from her family, she didn't tell them because they wouldn't understand anyway. She enjoyed the feeling and just let it flow.

Natalie began thinking about what someone had said to her the previous week. A church member that used to attend church with her and Jason came and spoke to her at the Apple Festival. He told her how much Natalie's life has improved, and that Jason was still with her. She did not feel like her life has improved, even though in hindsight, it probably had. Regardless, Natalie was depressed and being tortured daily by a senile old woman who blamed her for what her son did.

Natalie went to bed that night, trying to clear her head. "Is these feelings go away tomorrow, I'm going to say it's the change of the seasons." Natalie thought. next day, these feelings didn't go away. "What is going on?" Natalie asked herself as she sat down at the kitchen table. "Is something wrong with me?" She thought. She took a deep breath and tried to focus on other things. Throughout the week, Natalie's atmosphere change did not go away. She finally decided to open up to someone about it, her friend Patricia. She hesitated to reach out to her. Natalie's anxiety made her think that she was a bother to Patricia, but finally the strange feeling took over and she had no choice but to text her.

Natalie got her phone, and explained her situation, shanking. "Is this a change from God or is this an attack from the enemy? I feel like I'm just sitting and waiting for something bad to happen."

"There is a shift happening in you that is manifesting in the natural. Just let God continue to work from behind the scenes."

It was just a few days before Halloween. Natalie and Kelcie were left cleaning the house, preparing to cook dinner. Their parents were gone for the evening, so they were left to cook for themselves.

"Do we have any sauce for lasagna," Kelcie asked.

"I don't know, I think we do, but just in case, I think we should run to the store and get some," Natalie replied.

The rain was pouring outside, and Natalie grabbed an umbrella from the basket near the door. Kelcie chose to drive, looking for the keys.

Natalie was focused on herself and making leaps and bounds she never thought she would make. They made lasagna, as the rain pounded the windows. After Dinner, Natalie and her sister Kelcie decided to prepare for the holiday, like they did every year. Natalie did not feel much like celebrating, she was depressed. Natalie had lost her motivation during the day. She stopped wearing makeup, which was something she loved. She simply just did not feel like dealing with putting it on.

    Natalie and Kelcie were sitting in the living room floor, preparing Halloween candy in treat bags when Natalie's father ran in the house with news from a distant cousin.

"Did you hear that Dustin was in trouble with the state?" He asked.

"No. What are you talking about in trouble with the state?" She asked, confused.

"With the wreck. I reckon the state has the case, or at least that's what William told me."

Natalie's face lit up with joy "You mean they finally decided to start investigating it?" She asked. "How did William know?"

"Anywhere knowing him." Her father said.

"Dustin practically ran Jason down and killed him. He might as well have gotten a gun and shot him." William said.

Kelcie sat quietly for a few moments before speaking up. "You know, since you mention that. I did see Paul Howard and another man investigating the place where the wreck happened. They were out of their vehicles looking in the grass for something." She said.

Natalie became filled with joy and excitement. All the anger that she had felt towards Dustin was gone in an instant. Justice was about to be served, and the feeling was incredible. Natalie still had her doubts though about what William said to be true, so she sat and thought for a few minutes before deciding what to do. She got her phone and texted Blake, because if anything had happened, he would have known about it. "Hey Blake, did you hear about Dustin getting in trouble with the state?" Natalie's message said.

Natalie could not contain her excitement anymore, she got up and ran through the house. "I feel like singing." She said. "Thank you Lord for being a God of Justice." Eventually, Natalie calmed down and continued helping Kelcie.

"I swear, when I see Diana, I'm going to ask her about it." Kelcie said.

"I bet she's about to die. Especially since she paid all that money to have it covered up." Natalie said, laughing.

"I guarantee she is." Kelcie responded.

Natalie finished up her job and her excitement began to wear off, making her extremely tired. Natalie went to lay down and take a nap in her room until she found out more.

Chapter 16

"Our Father who art in heaven. Hallowed be thy name. Thy kingdom come, thy will be done on Earth as it is in heaven. Give us this day our daily bread and forgive us our trespasses as we forgive those who have trespassed against us. For thine is the kingdom and the power and the glory, forever. Amen"

"Amen," Natalie said in agreement with the congregation. She grabbed her purse from the floor and followed the large crowd of people into the vestibule. The first church service of 2020 had just ended and Natalie was excited for the upcoming year ahead.

Smiling, she walked into the vestibule in her green velvet dress and met up with her family to discuss going out to eat. "So where are we going?" She asked.

"Wherever everybody wants to go," her aunt responded.

Natalie walked over to her mother who was talking to the preacher about her upcoming surgery. Sitting at a table in a local restaurant, just after church let out on Sunday. She was not too keen on eating their, but the rest of her family chose to eat there, not giving her much of a choice. She with her aunt, her parents, sister and twin cousins. All that was on her mind was Wednesday. The day her mother was to go in a for a minor heart procedure. Kelcie spoke up out of how where and said "Hey sissy, what's your size of t-shirt?"

"Extra large, why?" Her aunt responded.

"Good, because I am going to put a picture of Natalie on the front of it and me and you are going to walk around the hospital in the shirts, advertising her to all the men," Kelcie said, making the whole table laugh.

"Are you saying I have no game?" Natalie questioned.

"Whatever you're doing definitely isn't working,"

Natalie bursted into laughter, knowing that she meant well, but it was also funny. Deep down inside of her, she just wished people would understand that she can not date until God speaks to her. She did not let it bother her, though. She continued on throughout the day, being her regular self. Around that time, an extremely tall man walked into the restaurant.

"Look a little harder Kelcie, does he have a ring on his hand?" Her aunt said.

"I don't think so! There you go Natalie, I've found you a man!" Kelcie exclaimed.

Natalie rolled her eyes and continued to focus on enjoying her meal. She knew they only meant it as a joke and that they were trying to lighten the mood a little bit, but it still hurt. She so badly wanted someone to laugh with her, to enjoy spending time with her.

During this time, Natalie's Faith was being tested. She knew that God was not going to abandon her, but the burden of being single was beginning to weigh on Natalie. God granted her with incredible faith for weeks and she still had faith during the down days, but the burden was heavy. She began to pray, daily whoever the burden would feel the heaviest. There was still no sign of improvement. "God has brought me too far to leave me," she told herself, motivating her to keep going.

Natalie left the restaurant with mixed emotions. She had faith, but was not seeing any movement. She thought she was doing something wrong. "God, what's the deal?" She thought as she sat down in the backseat of the car. She tried to keep positive knowing that whatever God promises comes to pass.

When she got home, she did not take her usual Sunday afternoon nap. Instead she packed her things to get ready to go to the hospital for her mother's surgery. Natalie did not know if they would be spending the night or not, but she wanted to be prepared. She also wanted things to keep herself busy in the waiting room.

Finally, the morning of surgery arrived. It was five in the morning and pitch black outside. The temperature was unusually warm and Natalie took her bed pillow in the car with her. Kelcie packed a phone charger, a bag of cookies, and a book of word searches to keep them busy while they waited. Natalie wore sweatpants and a t-shirt. Different than what she would usually wear and her hair was pulled up into a messy bun.

"You can't get a man looking like that!" Kelcie said when Natalie walked into the living room.

"Trust me, I don't intend on trying to find someone today. I'm way too tired," Natalie explained.

Both girls slept in the car on the way to Lexington. Natalie was thinking about everything. Her mind could not quite down. She turned her focus mostly on Jesus.

Praying that she would get some kind of breakthrough soon.

When they arrived at the waiting room, it was dark and dull. There were no windows and outdated wallpaper that looked like it was from the mid-90's. Natalie made herself comfortable in one of the chairs closest to the television as she waited for the rest of her family to show up. Natalie looked up and was surprised to see her church pastor show up to the hospital. He came over and sat down in front of them, having casual conversations.

Natalie's grandmother came in and sat down beside her.

"You know that cat of ours still doesn't have hair," she heard her father say.

"Yeah, that cat is dangerous though," Kelcie chimed in.

"Dangerous?" The pastor asked, confused.

"Yeah, we took that cat to the vet and he lost his mind," her grandmother said.

"Oh Lord, here we go," Natalie said as Kelcie laughed at her.

"That cat was jumping on shelves and knocking over everything. He bit the vet and then they tried to put him in a cage. He broke the cage," her grandmother continued.

That day felt like it would never end. Everyone was tired and just wanted to sleep. Natalie got bored and started doing crosswords and watched the president brief the nation. "I wish I had someone to talk to," Natalie thought. She texted Blake, hoping that he would respond to her. He responded, to Natalie's surprise. Tuesday in January. and she wanted to make herself as comfortable as possible while sitting in the waiting room.

Chapter 17

Brandon was hard at work, typing on his computer at his office desk. He leaned back and sighed, waiting for the extremely long day to come to an end. "Is this ever going to end," he thought after having a stressful day. He kept looking at the clock, praying for the day to hurry up and end. His black hair glistened in the hot August sun shining through his office window. He was lonely and going through a lot of emotions since his father passed away. Sooner rather than later, it was his break time. He came into the break room where all of his coworkers where are.

"Hey Brandon, could you get that phone call?"

"Yeah, of course," he agreed, as he sat there waiting on the phone call to come through.

He took the phone call and finished up his work for the day. It was nighttime and he had plans to go be with his friend after work. He put his paperwork into his briefcase and took the long walk to his car. He threw the paperwork inside and breathed a sigh of relief. He stuck the key into the ignition and began driving out of Huntington.

"How have you been doing? I know it's been rough on you," his friend asked, worried about him since his father died.

"Yeah, I'm doing alright. A lot better than I was," Brandon responded, not wanting to address the situation any further.

He redirected the conversation and informed him that he was coming over for a little while and that he was only a few minutes out. He hung up and began to relax a little bit. He kept driving and eventually pulled into his driveway. He got out of the car and made his way into his friend's home where he and his wife were sitting.

"Well, look who it is," his friend said, jokingly.

"Oh yeah right, you knew you were expecting me," Brandon said as he entered his home.

He sat down on the couch taking a break for a few moments and just collecting himself from the day. Once rested and after he finished chatting with them, he began examining his life. His heart still ached from the pain he had experienced. Somehow, the conversation got on to the topic of relationships.

"There's no good women left out there," He said.

"Of course there are, you just have to look," his friend reassured him.

"Oh that app is just for hookups and a good time," Brandon expressed.

"You never know, create a profile," his friend urged.

"Fine! But I'm only keeping it two weeks to prove my point,"

Brandon pulled his phone out of his pocket and began creating a profile.

"I'm telling you, this is useless man," he said.

"Oh come on, it's not that bad," his friend assured him once again.

Once finished, he collected himself and went home. He started swiping through the profiles and looking at all the women. He matched with a few, some of them were fake accounts and others just weren't really clicking with him. He got into bed and got cozy, eventually drifting off to sleep.

The next morning, the bright light shined through his bedroom window. He rose up out of bed and wiped the crust out of his eyes. His heart sank knowing that he had to go to work. He sighed and got out of bed stumbling into the bathroom to take a shower. He turned the water on and stared at himself in the mirror for a few moments.

As soon as he was finished he had plans to go to a bible study. Dating again is something that scared Brandon terribly after his nasty breakup from a manipulative woman. He wanted someone new, but was concerned about being left high and dry once again. "There's no good women left out there," he thought as he drove a post into the ground.

He considered online dating, but that almost never works out and was against it, Knowing that he didn't have many other options. He finished his work for the day and went to his parents house for dinner as he lived by himself. He walked into their home through the front door and sat down at the kitchen table, feeling a little down.

"What's wrong dear?" His mother asked, carrying things over to the table.

"Nothing, I'm just tired of being alone yet I'm scared to get back out there again," he explained.

He finished his dinner and drove home, where he fell down onto the couch. His mind was racing, but ultimately decided to go through with creating a dating profile. "Here we go," she sighed as he started setting everything up. In just a few minutes, he already had some matches, but none of them peaked his interest. He found one who he thought was cute, but in return just wanted his money and was only interested in making him subscribe to her only fans account.

Weeks went by and nothing was happening. He started to give up hope of ever finding anyone again. Each girl he matched with just wasn't clicking with him. Most weren't even real people. It seemed that he was always swiping left. Until one day he came across a profile. He stopped and looked at the beautiful redheaded woman in the photo. He was mesmerized by her. "She can't be real," he thought. He decided to try his luck and reached out to her.

"So what brings you to this wasteland?" He asked.

"I've been single for a while, and I'm looking for something serious," Natalie responded.

"Okay, she definitely can't be real," he thought and continued with the conversation.

Chapter 18

Natalie was enjoying life and not paying much attention to her singleness. All of sudden, she gets a notification on her phone from a guy named Brandon. Natalie was hesitant at first. She didn't know if she needed to respond or not. Out of curiosity, Natalie looked anyway. She picked up her phone and touched the notification.

"So what brings you to this wasteland?" The message read.

"I don't want to talk about it," Natalie responded.

"Ok, you don't have to. Are you sure you don't want to?" He asked once again.

Natalie was startled and a little confused. "Why is he speaking to me like this?" She thought. Responding to the messages as best she could. Getting tired, she ended the conversation.

"I hope we can talk tomorrow," she added as she left her phone behind.

Still confused, she knew that there was something different about him and was excited to hear back from him. She went to her room and turned the lights off, falling down on her bed. Her heart was beating fast, knowing that this could be different.

The next morning, Natalie was disappointed that she hadn't heard from Brandon. She brushed it off as him not being interested and just went on about her day. She came into the kitchen and filled up a glass with some fresh made lemonade. She plugged her printer up and printed out some worksheets for her to start writing on a brand new project. Natalie opened the blind in her room, spread her things out on the bed and began brainstorming ideas for her new project.

She wrote down everything she thought about. Her characters were designed to represent people of the past and famous historical characters. "It's so hot in here," she thought, fanning her face as she tried to cool down. her heart up to love again. A switch was flipped inside her brain and her soul began to fill with faith. She began her journey to finding love once again. She was so miserable, that she couldn't bear to be miserable anymore. Still crying in bed, Natalie sat up and dried her eyes. "The next guy that offers to take me on a date, I'm taking the offer," Natalie said, holding her tissue and looking up and the dark ceiling in her bedroom. She took a deep breath and laid back against her mint green pillow in bed. "I haven't slept in three days," she thought, almost pulling her hair out from stress.

Grabbing her phone, she signed up for an online dating service. She wanted to find someone and find someone fast. "Maybe I shouldn't do this, God did tell me to wait on him," she thought. She was tired of waiting on God. She waited for years, and her body began to feel paralyzed with fear.

    Natalie remembered the dream that God gave her just a few days prior. In the dream, She was sitting on a couch somewhere over in Johnson County. The man she was supposed to be with was there and she looked into his eyes. He was so tall and had dark black hair and pale skin. He was wearing a crucifix necklace around his neck, while wearing a suit. He hugged her with such force, and she felt so much love. It was hard for her to explain, but she had the warm fuzzy feeling inside of her again that she hadn't experienced in a long time. Natalie woke up for a moment and she still felt the love coming from that warm embrace. Natalie drifted back off to sleep and snapped back out of the dream that was given to her, but not forgetting about it.

"I need to focus," she thought, rolling over in bed and eventually falling asleep.

The next morning, Natalie woke up and felt so cozy and warm inside. She remembered the covenant that she made. "I'm going to go on a date with the next man that offers," she thought, and kept telling herself that. Giving herself a pep talk before she entered into this new phase of her life. Heart stopped in her chest upon realizing what she had said. "I'm so nervous," she thought, knowing how hard dating is. "Faith without works is dead," she reminded herself, believing that the next man who asked her on a date would be the one.

She got up and came into the living room excited about the new life change that was about to happen. The one thing she desired more than anything else in the world was finally at her fingertips. She was running on a high and didn't feel like it was going to collapse under her like the last times. Natalie was determined to push through this time of testing.

Natalie got her phone and looked at a few of the matches she had on her dating profiles. Even though she was in quarantine, she was determined to meet this man. She fell to the ground and prayed for God to open up opportunities for her to meet this man. "Is this really what I'm supposed to be doing?" She thought, hoping God would give her some insight into what was going on in her life. Naturally, by the end of May, Natalie was beginning to experience a little bit of discouragement. She wanted to be with someone so bad, but she just couldn't seem to find what she was looking for. Nothing felt right in her spirit and everything was off.

Discouragement started to creep in, "am I ever going to find someone again. I just want to love someone," she thought. Throwing her hands up in frustration. Each day, Natalie began to pray for a husband. Her faith was suffering, and so was her hope.

One late August night, she matched with someone. "Okay, he looks like a nice guy," she thought as she shrugged her shoulders. Thinking that he'd never reach out to her. About an hour later, Natalie felt her phone buzz. She looked down and Realized that Brandon had sent her a message. Still skeptical, she responded. "God hasn't spoken to me yet," she thought, feeling discouraged and on the verge of giving up.

"These are the strangest messages I've ever gotten in my life," she thought, trying to respond as best as she could.

Through only sharing a few text messages, Natalie knew that there was something different about him. Natalie talked to him back and forth for a few days. One night, he stopped completely. Natalie began to panic and just wrote it off as him not being interested in her.

"I guess I'll just have to keep looking," she thought as she got up off the couch and went to lay down in the bed.

The next morning came and the day went by slowly. Natalie felt alone, and she was nervous that he wasn't interested in her. "What did I do wrong?" she thought, as she tried her absolute best to focus on work and just get the day over. Then her phone buzzed. Natalie's face lit up, but she was still having doubts. "Is this Natalie?" The message read.

Natalie began to think her period of waiting would never end. It seemed like everything she did, there was no light at the end of the tunnel. One afternoon, Natalie went to town for a gathering with some family and friends. She was calm and focused on having a good time. "I can't have fun if I don't cut this negativity out," she thought. "Lord, give me strength to keep fighting the good fight of faith," she asked, as she got out of the car.

"Hi Natalie," someone said.

"Hi," she said, trying to avoid human interaction as much as possible.

Chapter 19

After talking back and forth for weeks, Brandon asked Natalie on a date. Her heart stopped, but she knew the question was coming sooner or later.

"I'd love to," she replied. Though she was nervous, she was excited. This guy genuinely seemed interested in her and she was ready to take that next step.

She went into the living room, her heart pounding and smiling from ear to ear. "I hope they don't notice me smiling like an idiot," she thought, knowing that her family would tease her if they found out. She was excited to actually be getting out of the house for once. She began mentally preparing herself for the date. Literally her first date since 2016.

She was nervous, thousands upon thousands of thoughts flooded her mind. "What if I mess this up?"

"What If he's still not the one?" "What happens if this one dies too?" She thought, staring at herself in the mirror.

Natalie was excited, but she was so nervous. Her mind kept going from one thing to another though the date was still a week away. The next day, Natalie finally mustered up the courage to go tell her parents what was happening. She sat them down and explained to them the situation. They were happy for her, but the teasing commenced and so did the questions.

"What's he like?" Her mother asked.

"He's a really sweet guy and he seems very genuine," Natalie answered.

Natalie smiled watching her parents talk about him. "Out of all the people in the world, this is the set of parents I get stuck with," she thought, laughing at how lucky she was to have been given such an amazing support system.

Finally, the day of the date had arrived. There had been a lot of discussion as to what they would do, so they decided to go to the lake for a walk. Natalie came into the living room that dark and rainy morning. She sat down and spoke with her grandmother who had come to visit.

"What are you gonna wear tonight?" She asked.

"I have no idea," she thought.

She was on cloud nine, even though she had a ton of stuff to do before she could actually get ready. Her sister was working on some homework and Natalie was used to help.

"I need your help Natalie!"

"What now?" Natalie asked.

Natalie finished up helping her sister with her homework and got up to go get ready. She put on a yellow floral dress and got in her car and headed over to the Paintsville Lake. He was already there, waiting on her Just looking him made her heart skip a beat.

"Hey! I just wanted to tell you, don't be nervous,"

"Is it that obvious?" She asked, giggling.

"Yeah it is, but it's okay," he reassured her.

"So tell me more about yourself," he said.

"There's not much more to tell, I'm pretty boring," she said, laughing.

Natalie was so nervous, but even looking at his face made her feel like she was at home. Talking to him was easy, it was like he had known him all of her life. His jet black hair glistened in the late summer evening sun. His short beard was neatly groomed and he was well put together.

"Why don't you tell me more about you?" She asked as they started walking

"Well, I consider myself to be quite the comedian, or at least that's what my little brother tells me. I also have a puppy, girls like puppies right?" He asked, looking lovingly into Natalie's eyes.

Several times throughout their walk, Natalie noticed he was looking at her. Th She felt awkward as there was a long period of silence between the two of them. The conversation quickly changed when Brandon broke the ice.

"So tell me something about you that I don't know," he said.

"I don't know, I'm not that interesting," she responded

"Oh come on, there's definitely something that you've not told me,"

"Probably, but I can't think of it now,"

Both of them sat down on a bench for a break. Brandon shared things about his past and Natalie shared things about hers. She laughed at his crazy stories and the things he got himself into when he was younger.

They talked so long that they began to loose track of time. They looked up and just happened to realize it was getting dark.

"Hey, we should probably head back. It's getting dark," Natalie said.

"Yeah, you're right," he agreed.

They started walking back and the trail was darker than she thought it would be. With each step, it seemed like it was getting darker and she started to get scared. Brandon noticed and put his arm around her to comfort her. Natalie blushed and felt so much love in the way he put his arm around her.

"Oh my God I haven't felt this in so long," she thought.

Finally, they made it off the trail that seemed like it would never end. The street lights made Natalie relax since she could finally see where she was going. He walked her back to his car and they sat down and talked some more. They had great chemistry together. One was equally as interested as the other. Natalie was shocked at the amount of things they had in common. Everything from grief to their birthdays being in the same month.

"I hate to end this, but I should probably head home. It's getting late," she said.

"Okay, I'll walk you back to your car,"

They walked back to the car and stood for a few minutes. Brandon grabbed her hand and pulled her in close before she opened her car door.

"Can I have a kiss?" He asked.

"Yeah," she agreed and he leaned in and kissed her. She became weak kneed and couldn't stand very well. Her heart was racing at the thoughts of what just happened.

In the back of Natalie's mind, she felt guilty, but she knew Jason would want her to be happy.

Chapter 20

Natalie and Brandon had been talking for a while. After their first date, they had grown considerably closer. One cool evening in September, they were taking a walk in the park. Children were playing in the background and Brandon put his arm around Natalie. "I know what we can do," he said, as he grabbed a hammock out of the back of his car.

They walked and found two trees in the park, and put up the hammock. Natalie got in beside him, with her heart pounding. He put his arm around her and she laid her head on his chest.

"I never thought I'd have this again," she thought, while looking up at him and smiled.

Natalie got comfortable and enjoyed the moment. She wrapped her arms around him and started giggling with joy.

"What are you laughing at?" Brandon asked.

"Nothing," she responded.

"Tell me," he said, being flirty.

"I promise it's nothing,"

"Oh come on! Do you really expect me to believe that? Tell me what you're thinking,"

Realizing that he wasn't going to give in, Natalie opened up her mind and heart to him. She shared things that would have otherwise never been mentioned if he hadn't asked. They talked for hours about their lives and how much they cared for one another. Natalie was in pure bliss. The moment couldn't have been more perfect.

Soon, Natalie was completely in his arms. She giggles once again.

"What is it?" He asked

"I'm not telling you," Natalie said jokingly.

"You're really gonna do this to me again," he said as he put his face closer to hers.

"Yes," she giggled.

"Tell me or kiss me,"

Natalie kissed him and caught him off guard. He kissed her again and she smiled.

"Okay, now tell me,"

"That wasn't part of the deal," Natalie giggled

Darkness began to fall, and so did the temperature. Natalie started to get cold, but kept it to herself. She didn't want to leave that spot next to him. Her mind was racing and full of thoughts. "What if this isn't the one," she thought, worried about having her heart broken again. She laid back, out her long red hair over the hammock and looked up at the beautiful night sky. There wasn't a single cloud. She looked over at

Brandon and smiled. "I'm very lucky," she thought as she laid there, soaking in the moment. Brandon grabbed her by the waist and pulled her in closer to him. It startled her a little bit.

"What are you doing?" She asked, giggling and being taken off guard by the gesture.

"This," he said as kissed her cheek under the large oak tree.

Natalie's breath wasn't taken away. She sat there in complete shock, gazing at his face as if he had done something otherworldly.

"I'm sorry, I just couldn't wait any longer,"

"Why are you apologizing?" She interrupted, grinning from ear to ear.

It was getting late, and Natalie was freezing. She got up and wrapped herself up in the blanket he had given her as they made the long walk back to the car. As they were walking, he put his arm around her waist and held her as they walked.

Natalie felt whole. Completely filled and happy, something she never thought would happen again. Her heart raced as he smiled at her. She got back into his car and realized that her makeup was an absolute mess. Mascara was underneath her eyes as they started the long drive home.

"Hey, I want you to know something," Natalie spoke up.

"What is it?" He asked.

A little hesitant, Natalie spoke up and started talking about her last relationship and Jason's death. Natalie explained what happened to Jason and the things she saw the night he died.

Brandon looked over at Natalie, his heart breaking for her. He stretched his hand out and picked hers up and started rubbing his thumb over her hand.

"I'm sorry you had to go through that," he said, trying to comfort her.

"I'm surprised that I didn't break down," Natalie spoke up, genuinely shocked that she didn't break down.

Natalie smiled and realized how truly lucky she was. Finally, she was in a place that she wanted to be. Several thoughts went through her mind, and she was worried about him driving all the way back home since he lived two hours away. He pulled into Natalie's driveway, and they sat and talked for a few minutes. "So do I get a 3rd date?" He asked.

"Of course! That was a stupid question," Natalie responded, laughing.

"I mean, you never know,"

"Oh stop," Natalie said reassuring him that he had nothing to worry about.

He looked at her and smiled, full of love for this woman he barely knew. Everything about her was beautiful, her body, her soul, and her looks in general. "She's so out of my league. I wonder why she even likes me," he thought, as he leaned in for a final kiss.

"I don't want you to go," Natalie said.

"That's really sweet," he said, listening as those words reached deep inside of his soul. She really liked him and knew this relationship was going to go somewhere.

"I cannot believe this," Natalie thought, looking at him as in the moonlight. Natalie had not been cared for like this in a long time. He was so soft spoken and patient. With everything he did, she fell deeper in love with him.

A couple weeks later, Natalie was starting to worry about how interested in her he was. They had their third date, and he still hadn't shown any signs of asking her to be his girlfriend. She was ready to take that step, but he obviously wasn't.

It was the beginning of October, and the nights were getting longer. One night, after Brandon had gotten off work, he had an idea. "I wonder if Natalie would go on a weekend getaway with me," he thought, seeing how stressed she was. Natalie agreed and started thinking about the places they would go.

The next week, Natalie decided where she wanted to go. A place where she always wanted to go, but didn't. "I want to go to the Cumberland Falls to see the moonbow," she texted.

"Okay, we can do that," Brandon responded.

Natalie arranged for him to meet her parents shortly after making this decision. She wanted him to meet them the day they were supposed to leave. Parent meetings were always nerve wracking for her, because she never knew what they would say or do to embarrass her. "What if they don't approve of him?" She thought, even though she knew that was unlikely.

The morning of the trip arrived, she got up early and got herself ready. It was nine in the morning and she was exhausted, and nervous. She came into the living room that morning, feeling uneasy but excited. She put on a gray sweatshirt and a little bit of makeup. She didn't feel like dressing up to travel.

Natalie was on cloud nine, but she also had her guard up. She was still afraid of loosing him. She sat down at the breakfast table and took a deep breath. Brandon was supposed to be there supposed to be there at one o'clock, she kept watching the clock on the wall above their vintage buffet table. She's known him for two months, and she had a feeling that their relationship was about to take a major turn.

Natalie's stomach was aching from nervousness. Her parents were getting ready to meet him and left her alone for a few moments. One o'clock came faster than she thought. It's like she looked up and the time was different.

"Just pulled in," Brandon texted.

Natalie's heart starting pounding as she watched him walk to the front door. It was pouring the rain so he took his shoes off at the door.

"Hey," he said as she let him in the door.

"Hi,"

Natalie's parents stood up and greeted him, shaking his hand. Brandon was nervous than she was. In his previous relationships, meeting the parents didn't always go so great.

"It's nice to meet you," her mom said, breaking the silence.

"It's nice to meet you too,"

"So, Natalie tells me you're from Ohio,"

"Yeah, that's right, I am"

Natalie looked at him with nervousness as they chatted about his career. He was a business analyst for a major company and had a lot of funny stories.

Natalie looked over at Brandon and smiled. "Are you ready to go?" She asked.

"Yeah, I am," he answered, bending down to pick up her stuff and carry it to the car.

Natalie followed behind him and mentally prepared herself for the long car ride. She sat down in the car stared at his dark black hair underneath a baseball cap. thinking about how lucky she was. He made her so happy in ways that Jason didn't, but she loved both of them. She found herself comparing the two men often. Natalie felt guilty for comparing Brandon to Jason because he was so much more than a replacement. The love she felt for him was different than the love she had for Jason.

He had great respect for Jason and that made Natalie love him even more.

Chapter 21

Brandon woke up, still laying in bed, he looked up at the ceiling and thought about Natalie. "How did I fall for this woman so fast," he thought looking over at the beautiful woman in the bed next to him. He was mesmerized by her. It was deeper than just her beauty. Natalie was a different woman all together. He admired her for how she overcame so much.

He got up and walked over to her bed. "Good morning beautiful," he whispered to Natalie. Just thinking about her made his heart flutter. "I really want to be with this woman," he thought as Natalie started to wake up.

He looked at her and smiled, thinking about the day they had planned together. They were going to see the waterfall and then out to eat.

"Get ready, we've got a lot to do today," he said nervously, knowing that he was about to ask Natalie to be his girlfriend. He noticed that something was a little different with Natalie. She didn't seem like herself.

"What's going on?" He asked.

"I'm just tired, I didn't sleep good last night," Natalie responded.

"I told you to wake me up if you couldn't sleep!"

"You and I both know I wasn't going to do that," Natalie said, laughing.

The night before, they weren't able to see the moonbow for the rain. Brandon was going to ask her if they saw it, but they didn't. So he had plans to take her back. The two of them got in the car and headed towards the waterfall. He was so nervous, but tried to hide it the best way he could.

"Has she noticed yet?" He thought.

He parked the car and opened the door for Natalie, getting the umbrella out of the back of the car in case it rained. Natalie bundled herself up in her pink jacket and they walked the long pathway to get to the waterfall. They stood there for a few minutes, and he noticed that Natalie was shivering.

"Are you cold?" He asked

"Yeah, I'm freezing," Natalie responded, so he pulled her in towards him and put his arm around her.

"This waterfall is a lot bigger in daylight," he said as he held on to her.

Brandon got tense and started thinking about ways he could ask her to be his girlfriend. "I'm just going to do it, but I'll let her bring it up first," he thought. He stared off into the distance and got quite, hoping to get Natalie's attention.

"What are you thinking so hard about?" She asked, feeling how tense he was.

"Are you sure you want to know what I'm thinking about?"

"Well yeah, I wouldn't have asked if I didn't want to know," she responded.

    Brandon took a deep breath and put both his arms around her, pulling her in even closer.

"I was thinking that this waterfall would be a good place for me to ask you to be my girlfriend," he said.

    Natalie looked up at him and smiled with pure joy. "Did you honestly expect me to say no?" She asked, leaning in for a kiss. He rubbed her back and relaxed his tense shoulders.

"Yeah, I did. I didn't know if you thought it was too soon or if you weren't ready,"

"Of course I was ready. I've waited on you to ask me that for a long time," she said, as he held her closer to his chest.

His shirt was soaked with mist from the waterfall and misty rain. Natalie finally started to breathe normally again from all the excitement and decided to leave.

"You're my girlfriend now," he said with a smile on his face as he sat down in the car and buckled his seatbelt.

"Yes, you are," she said, beaming with absolute joy.

Brandon had never felt love towards a woman like her before. He considered himself to be lucky that this woman chose him out of all the men she could have had.

"You know you can do so much better than me, right?" He asked.

"How could I possibly do any better?" She asked.

"You deserve way more than I can ever give you," Brandon said.

This was the beginning of a new journey for the both of them. Both who were previously wounded and broken souls from the after affects of death were brought together by the grace of God for healing and companionship.

I'd like to acknowledge the hard work put in by my entire team of people. A huge thank you to my alpha reader, A huge thank you to my alpha reader Kendra Boersen, my beta reader Samone Johnson, and my editor Sam Wright.

Made in the USA
Columbia, SC
08 March 2021